Praise for

Help! I'm an Alien

'[A] crazy, hilarious adventure [and]
one of the most entertaining books you
will read this year.'
Lancashire Evening Post

'This is a fast-paced page turner
with a laugh on every page.'
Goodreads

'Very impressive writing in one of the funniest
opening chapters that I've read this year.'
The Bookbag

'Daniel is a funny character, self-aware [and]
the pace of the narrative is perfectly pitched
to keep the reader interested
and entertained.'
The Book Activist

JO FRANKLIN

Illustrated
by Aaron Blecha

troika books

For Cedric and Eleanor

First published in the UK by TROIKA BOOKS
Well House, Green Lane, Ardleigh CO7 7PD, UK
www.troikabooks.com

First published 2017

Text copyright © Jo Franklin 2017
Illustrations copyright © Aaron Blecha 2017

A CIP catalogue record for this book is available
from the British Library

ISBN 978-1-909991-42-2

1 2 3 4 5 6 7 8 9 10

Printed in Poland

1

Things You Need to Know About My Family's Brains

All my family are complete and utter brainiacs, except me. I don't know how I ended up being a Kendal, but I'm too young to leave home so I guess I'll have to get on with it.

Dad is a university lecturer. He teaches brainy people how to be even brainier about brains. He's something called a neuroscientist but don't ask me what it means because I am not one of his students.

Dad keeps his brain on top of the fridge. Not his actual brain, that's in his skull (I think). The brain on top of the fridge is plastic and breaks in half so you can look inside. The company that made Dad's brain labelled the different parts with weird names.

Dad tried to explain what they meant, so I added
my own labels to help me to remember.

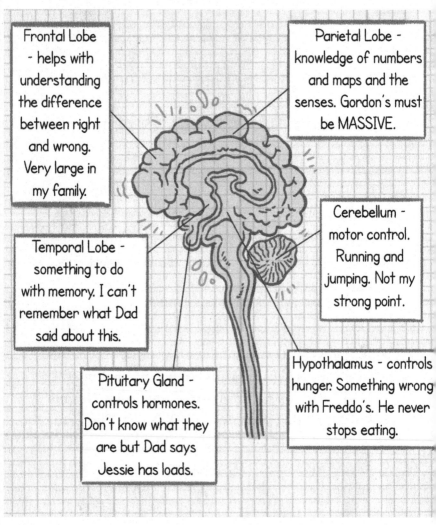

Frontal Lobe
- helps with
understanding
the difference
between right
and wrong.
Very large in
my family.

Parietal Lobe -
knowledge of numbers
and maps and the
senses. Gordon's must
be MASSIVE.

Cerebellum -
motor control.
Running and
jumping. Not my
strong point.

Temporal Lobe -
something to do
with memory. I can't
remember what Dad
said about this.

Pituitary Gland -
controls hormones.
Don't know what they
are but Dad says
Jessie has loads.

Hypothalamus - controls
hunger. Something wrong
with Freddo's. He never
stops eating.

Mum isn't a brain expert but she knows everything about everything else. She works as a school receptionist (not at my school, thank goodness) and knows every kid's name, their favourite colour and what size pants they wear, although she wouldn't admit it. She also knows all the parents' secrets because she reads the head teacher's emails. The parents call her The Dobermann. She thinks it's funny.

So do I.

Mum is very fierce and she has a keen sense of smell. She always barks at my best friend Freddo when he smuggles a bag of chips into my bedroom. (No food upstairs. One of her rules.) So Freddo and I call her Dober-Mum. I don't call her that to her face as I don't think she will find *that* very funny and I'm scared she might bite me.

My incredibly annoying older sister, Jessie, acts like she knows everything. Actually, she only knows everything about One Dimension, who are her favourite band. But as it's the only thing she ever wants to talk about, she is a brainiac in her own world.

Timmy is only two years old. I think it's fair to say he's not a brainiac yet. However he does know how to get his own way. Especially with Dad.

If Timmy wants something and Dad says, 'No', Timmy clamps his mouth shut and stops breathing. First he turns red, then he turns white. He would turn blue next but Dad panics because stopping breathing starves the brain of oxygen and kills off zillions of brain cells. So Dad gives Timmy exactly what he wants.

That leaves me, Daniel, aged ten. My growth decided to concentrate on my body, not my brain. So I'm very tall but not very clever.

Mum and Dad are disappointed that I do not share their brainpower. Last Christmas they bought me a book called *A Million Amazing Facts Boys Should Know*. I still don't know any of the amazing facts because I use the book to prop up the wonky leg on my bed.

Both my parents are very competitive about being brainy and race to answer the questions on *Mastermind* and *University Challenge*. There's no point me joining that race. I'd lose every time. Instead I am competitive with my best friend Freddo about being a NOT-brainiac.

Freddo normally gets the lowest marks in any test at school. He's really proud of it. I try to do as badly as him but I've never managed it yet. Maybe I've inherited one or two brain cells after all.

Freddo and I are compiling a list of NOT-brainiac words. We're hoping to find one for each letter of the alphabet. So far we've only got these ones:

F – Fool
I – Idiot
M – Moron
N – Ninny

But today, for the first time ever, I learnt something new and I found out about it before Mum.

I was about to leave for school when the post arrived. A really thick envelope dropped through the letter box. It was addressed to Dad and had a USA stamp. I was about to ask him what it was when Dad snatched the letter out of my hand.

'Don't tell Mum!' he said. 'It's a secret surprise.'

At that moment, Mum came down the stairs with Timmy. Dad stuffed the letter up the back of his jumper.

'Time for school, Dan,' Mum said. Then she stopped in her tracks, put Timmy down, grabbed my shoulders and did her mind-reading Dober-Mum trick of staring into my eyes to find out what I was up to.

What I was up to was trying to keep Dad's USA surprise a secret. But the United States of America is a very big place and my brain is very small, and the secret was desperate to escape.

'I'm late,' I said and ducked out of her fierce Dober-Mum claws and dashed out the door.

I hope Dad tells her (and me) the secret really soon or my tiny brain will explode.

2

The Trouble
With Crisps

As I walked to school I kept wondering what the letter from the USA could be about. Mum wants to go on holiday to the States but Dad doesn't like flying so we never go anywhere that involves an aeroplane. Mum sent him on a Fear of Flying hypnosis course, so maybe he's got over his hang-up and booked a holiday to the USA as a surprise.

We could all go on a yee-hah cowboy holiday.

We could get in the Guinness book of records by cleaning every window on the Empire State Building in a day.

Or we could walk across the Grand Canyon blindfolded.

But where I really want to go to is Florida to visit all the brilliant theme parks like Disneyworld and Universal Studios. And it's sunny all the time so Mum would love it.

I reckon Dad is taking us to Florida. This is going to be the best holiday ever!

There was a lot of shouting in my classroom as I opened the door.

'More! More! More!' everyone chanted but I couldn't see what they wanted more of as there was a load of open umbrellas in the way.

'I suggest you protect yourself, Mr Kendal.' Gordon the Geek, my second best friend, stood just inside the door. He was wearing a long, plastic tourist rain poncho over his blazer. It looked like he was having a baby.

Gordon is a neat

freak as well as a geek and goes to extreme lengths not to get dirty, but I hadn't seen this outfit before.

'What's going on?' I said.

'I have had to make my own hazmat suit,' he said. 'Until my order for a Shield-Max Level-A fully-encapsulating suit with built-in respirator is delivered. It withstands anthrax, sarin and radioactivity. I will be able to seal myself in and survive for three hours.'

'Why do you need to cover up?'

Gordon pointed a shaky finger at the mob of kids who were still chanting.

'Eat! Eat! Eat!' Everyone stamped their feet and slammed their hands on the desks. I jumped up onto a chair, hoping to see what was going on.

Freddo and Rooners, the football captain, were face to face, shoving crisps in their mouths. The floor was littered with empty crisp packets.

Rooners' and Freddo's cheeks were bulging, their faces covered in greasy, salty crumbs.

Another crisp-eating competition! When would Rooners give up? Freddo was the Crispmeister. He likes to make out he's laid back, but actually Freddo is the most competitive person I know.

Freddo licked his lips and swallowed hard. He grabbed another handful of crisps and shoved them in his mouth.

'Freddo is now in the lead!' Spike shouted.

Rooners' cheeks grew bigger as he tried to move his mouthful of fried potatoes and additives to the back of his throat. His shoulders heaved and his face turned green.

Gordon sunk down under his hazmat rain poncho in the farthest corner of the classroom.

Someone opened a packet of cheese and onion and shoved it under Rooners' nose. Rooners clamped his hand over his mouth and looked around the room with bulbous eyes.

Freddo was still chomping but it didn't look good. His whole body wobbled like a demented washing machine as he tried to swallow his mouthful.

That was the moment Mr Pitdown came in.

'What is going on?' Our teacher tugged the corner of his moustache. The room fell silent except for Freddo chomping and Rooners spluttering.

The crisp-eating contestants paused for a moment, closed their eyes and stood perfectly still.

'Please sit down. I have an important announcement to make.'

Freddo's and Rooners' eyes snapped open at exactly the same time and a volcano of crisp confetti exploded out of their mouths.

3

Tested to
Destruction

'What the –?' There are some words that mean instant dismissal for any teacher. Unfortunately, Mr Pitdown stopped himself from saying one of them just in time.

'Sorry about that, sir,' Rooners said.

Freddo shoved the crisp crumbs with his foot in a feeble attempt to hide them under the desk.

Mr Pitdown wasn't fooled. His face had gone so stony he could have auditioned for a part as a gargoyle. He ordered Freddo to fetch a broom.

'This is a disappointing start to the day,' he said as he paced across the front of the classroom, watching Freddo and Rooners clear up.

Everyone expected Mr Pitdown to erupt into an ugly firework display. But luckily for us he had something else on his mind.

'I've got an exciting quiz for you to do. This is your opportunity to become the school representative for this year's National Brainiac Championship.'

Freddo looked across the classroom and rolled his eyes at me. I rolled my eyes back. It wasn't going to be either of us. That was certain.

'This quiz is set by some of the brainiest people in the country. Mr Biggend asked the teachers to come up with some questions to be considered by the quiz masters. He sent them off to Brainiac HQ and I'm pleased to say that my question was selected to be included in the quiz.

Question One was set by me.' He stroked his moustache and smiled like a snake.

Actually, I don't know if snakes can smile but I bet they look smug sometimes, even if they don't have a stupid moustache.

The rest of the class buzzed with enthusiasm.

Rooners grinned at Spike and they exchanged a thumbs-up sign.

Susan Albright sharpened her pencil.

I don't know why they thought they stood a chance. There was only going to be one winner.

Gordon stood up, took his rain poncho off and folded it carefully before slipping it into his briefcase with his laptop. He adjusted his chair and placed his hands on the desktop. He lightly danced his fingertips over the surface of the desk as if he was still at the computer keyboard. He was ready.

'This is a privilege,' Mr Pitdown said as he clacked up the aisles, handing out the test papers.

'This is a total waste of time,' I hissed to Freddo as he sat back down.

Freddo had his fingers in his mouth, poking around at the back of his teeth for relics of his crispy victory. He still looked green, hardly in the best shape to do a test. He was bound to do even worse than normal.

But I was not put off. This was the perfect chance for me to beat Freddo in our own personal NOT-brainiac competition without getting into trouble

at home. Dober-Mum and Dad didn't need to know about the stupid championship. They couldn't be disappointed I scored badly when they wouldn't know I'd even taken the test. It was now or never. For the first time ever, I was going to do worse than Freddo.

'You have half an hour to answer these questions. Most are multiple choice. Some are one word or figure answers. Turn your papers over.'

Freddo and I exchanged the thumbs-down signs. We turned over the paper at exactly the same time.

Rat's bum! I knew the answer to the first question.

What is the middle name of James T Kirk, the captain of the Starship Enterprise *in* Star Trek?

Freddo and I like *Star Trek*, vintage and recent, but we've never told Mr Pitdown and we don't go around wearing plastic Spock ears. The question was easy.

Freddo looked across and gave me the Vulcan 'Live long and prosper' sign.

He ticked the paper with a flourish.

The choice of answers were:

A. *Tiberius*   B. *Trevor*
C.*Trekkie*   D.*Timothy*

It was definitely Tiberius. But I hesitated to tick the box.

These are the things I was thinking:

• If I ticked the wrong answer, I would be telling everyone I didn't know the middle name of my hero, Captain Kirk.

• If I ticked the right answer, Mr Pitdown might realise I liked *Star Trek* and want to be my friend.

• I wanted to get a lower score than Freddo really badly.

One of the brain cells I had inherited from Dad woke up at that moment and gave me an idea.

I ticked *A. Tiberius* and filled in all the other answers on the paper randomly without even looking at the questions properly. I either ticked a box or scribbled some random word or number down.

I knew I might get some of them accidently right but it didn't matter. My solution was foolproof.

Mr Pitdown has this stupid rule. No name. No score. I didn't put my name on the test paper which would mean an instant disqualification.

I was guaranteed to get a big fat zero.

4

Test

'How badly do you think you did?' I asked Freddo when Mr Pitdown let us out for break.

'Badly,' he said.

'Me too.'

'I bet I did worse,' Freddo said.

'Bet you didn't,' I said.

'Bet I did.'

'What do you want to bet?' I said.

'Ten pounds,' Freddo said.

That was five weeks' pocket money for me. But it was only one week's for Freddo.

One of the things I'm always going on about to Mum and Dad is the microscopic amount of pocket money I get.

'Freddo gets ten pounds a week,' I told them. 'And his mum and dad buy him whatever he wants whenever he wants it.'

'Freddo's dad is a market trader,' Dad said. 'He can get everything at cost price, which is way cheaper than in the shops.'

'What does Freddo spend his money on?' Dober-Mum said. 'Chips!'

'He likes chips,' I said. 'They make him happy. I can never be happy because if I spend my two pounds on one very small portion of chips, I'd have nothing left for the rest of the week.'

'Then don't buy chips,' Mum said and left the room.

'If I cancel my subscription to *The Beano*, can I have the money instead?' I asked Dad.

'No.'

'Why not?'

'*The Beano* might only be a comic but at least you read it,' Dad said. 'You can't read chips.'

And once again that had been the end of the 'I need more pocket money' conversation.

'I bet you ten pounds I get a lower score than you,' Freddo said.

'You're on!' I said. This was going to be the easiest ten pounds I had ever earned.

'Where's Gordon?' Freddo said as he slipped some coins into the vending machine.

'Making plans to travel to the National Brainiac Championship, I guess,' I said.

Freddo ran his finger over the buttons on the vending machine.

'I'm not sure I like crisps any more.' Freddo winced as he rubbed his stomach.

'Mars bar?' I suggested. There were plenty of other options in the vending machine.

'Might rot my teeth,' he said.

'Won't make your breath stink, though.'

'True but stinking breath is one of my personality traits. If a blind friend met me in the street and I smelt of Mars bars, they wouldn't recognise me.'

'I didn't know you had any blind friends.'

'Let me rephrase that. If I bumped into Gordon when he wasn't wearing his glasses, he wouldn't recognise me.'

'True,' I said.

'I'm switching to Hula Hoops.' Freddo punched the button and a red packet dropped out of the machine.

Gordon walked out of our classroom, his laptop suspended around his neck with a string and his eyes fixed on the open screen as he walked towards us. Mr Pitdown followed him.

'Well done, Gordon.' Our saddo teacher patted Gordon on the back and casually rested his arm across his shoulders.

'Wait for it!' I grabbed Freddo and pulled him to one side. 'Prepare yourself for a Geek eruption any second now!'

Gordon stood stock still, his face screwed up as if he'd walked into a cloud of tear gas. His eyelids flickered as his chest heaved.

'I look forward to seeing your score.' Mr Pitdown drummed his fingers on Gordon's shoulder before sauntering away with the bundle of test papers under his arm.

Gordon shivered as if a Hogwarts ghost had walked right through him. Instead of exploding, he fumbled in his pocket and pulled out a tiny aerosol. He sprayed a disinfectant mist around himself, then squirted each shoulder in turn until his blazer was damp.

There is no official uniform at our school but

Gordon insists on looking smart. He was wearing his pretend school blazer, a shirt, tie and no doubt a vest but, as far as he was concerned, he had been touched by a fellow human. It was going to take him at least three hours to get over it.

It was clear Mr Pitdown was not a brainiac. Even Freddo and I knew not to touch Gordon.

5

The School
Brainiac Is . . .

We had a special Year 6 assembly at the end of the day. Mr Biggend, the head teacher, stood on the stage and looked over all our heads towards the back wall of the hall.

'The National Brainiac Championship,' he pronounced the words very clearly, 'was inaugurated in 1977. I am proud to say the name Biggend is the very first to be engraved on the shield, because, children, I was the first ever National Brainiac Champion.'

'Biggend or Bighead?' I hissed to Freddo.

'Every year I have longed to have a student worthy of entering the competition. Entering and failing would mean certain humiliation for the contestant, for the school and . . .' he cleared his throat '. . . for me.' His mouth extended sideways and a row of teeth appeared under his nose. Mr Biggend was smiling.

'Someone call a doctor,' I said.

'Every year since I became a teacher I have entered my Year 6 pupils into this national competition. Every year I have hoped that someone would score one hundred per cent in this fiendish examination and would therefore be selected to compete in the final. Every year I have been disappointed. Until now. This year I am hoping to be able to hold the National Brainiac Championship shield in my hands again. Because, dear Year 6 . . .' Mr Biggend spread his arms wide and closed his eyes.

'Who's he talking to?' Freddo said.

'Himself,' I said. 'He's looking at the inside of his eyelids.'

'. . . for the first time in my teaching career we have a brainiac in our midst. One of you scored one hundred per cent.'

A murmur of disbelief rippled through the hall. One or two kids nudged each other. A few shook their heads.

Freddo twitched his head in Gordon's direction. Gordon adjusted his tie and straightened his blazer.

'I am very pleased to announce the winner and this school's representative for the National Brainiac Championship. After you have congratulated him you can go home, but in the meantime . . .' Mr Biggend at last looked at us kids sitting on the floor in front of him. His eyes scanned the rows of faces, looking for his brainiac.

'Stand up, mate,' Freddo called across to Gordon. 'Let's get this over with.'

Gordon blinked his eyes rapidly, which was a sign that he was pointedly ignoring Freddo. There was no way he'd stand up until Mr Biggend called his name.

'Congratulations to our brainiac.' Mr Biggend referred to the paper in his hand. 'Daniel Kendal.'

6

No! No! No!

What the `. . . ?

The whole of Year 6 turned to look at me.

Me? A brainiac? How did that happen? What about my no-name-on-the-test-paper foolproof plan? I hadn't even read the questions on that stupid test paper. I answered the questions randomly. I must have got the whole lot accidentally correct. My stomach clenched into the worst granny-knot ever and I thought I was going to be the third person to throw up in school today.

The room erupted into applause. And everyone from my class stood up and cheered. Everyone except my two best friends.

Gordon didn't flinch but his eyeballs bulged out of his eye sockets and his lips disappeared into the thin slit that used to be his mouth.

'You owe me ten pounds, you lying swot-face. You

wanted to win all along. There never was a NOT-brainiac competition,' Freddo said as he shoved me in the back and stormed past me. 'I only answered all the questions wrong for you!'

I wasn't supposed to win! I was supposed to beat Freddo and score zero.

'I AM a NOT-brainiac like you,' I shouted after him but he was so furious he didn't hear me.

I felt very lonely even though I was in a packed school hall with a load of cheering kids. I'd always been a NOT-brainiac. And now I was a NOT-brainiac with NO friends. What a disaster!

The other disaster was that I now owed Freddo five weeks' pocket money. A bet is a bet and Freddo would expect me to pay him, and I wasn't sure Freddo was in the mood to wait five weeks for his tenner now we weren't friends.

And Gordon was never going to forgive me for taking his place. He was way more a brainiac than me.

'Well done, Dan!' Rooners slapped me on the back as he passed. 'Didn't know you had it in you. You available for extra homework?'

'No!'

'I'll pay you.'

This was unbelievable! Rooners was prepared to hand over cash if I did his homework. Not only was he totally mad to trust me given my track record of being a NOT-brainiac, but it was cheating. I'd never even asked Gordon to do my homework for me and he is my second best friend.

'Do your homework yourself!' I felt my face flush with indignation. I thought Rooners was a sportsman not a cheat.

'My money not good enough for you?' Rooners shrugged and walked away.

I didn't know how to answer. I needed the money to pay Freddo, but I didn't want to be involved in a homework-cheating scam, however much Rooners paid me.

Mr Biggend pushed his way through the throng of cheering people and shook my hand.

'Other teachers wanted to disqualify you because . . . ahem,' he put his hand in front of his mouth and whispered, 'you forgot to write your name on the paper. But with a perfect score, I was prepared to overlook that tiny error. Kenny Daniels, I'm so proud of you.'

I didn't know what to be more annoyed about. The failure of my foolproof plan or Mr Biggend getting my wrong name.

'The National Brainiac Championship will lead to big things. It is an elite competition. Very few schools enter and only a select few get through to the final. This year National Brainiac Champion, next year *University Challenge*. Then *Mastermind*. Next thing you know you will be an Egghead. I always wanted to be an Egghead.' He looked out of the window and shook his head sadly.

I didn't know what he was talking about. How could entering a general knowledge quiz lead anywhere? Especially as I wasn't a brainiac, a mastermind or an egghead.

'When you win, we will celebrate. Instead of the Maths Day I was planning at the end of term, we'll have a party.'

The other kids who were still in earshot cheered.

'Nice one, Dan!'

'Awesome!'

They kept slapping me on the arm because I am too tall for them to pat me on the shoulder.

'What next for you, Kenny?' Mr Biggend patted

me on the back.

'Home,' I said. My legs were trembling and I was worried I was going to pass out. I needed to get some fresh air.

'Of course, what was I thinking? Go home, my boy. Go home and tell your family. Children!' Mr Biggend shouted out. 'Make way for the Mighty Brainiac.'

The crowd parted and everyone clapped as I stumbled towards the door. Mr Pitdown stood in the doorway, his arms folded firmly across his chest.

'Daniel,' he said and he raised his left eyebrow so high it disappeared into the wrinkles on his forehead. 'I don't know how you did it.'

Neither did I.

'I look forward to seeing how well you do against the REAL brainiacs at the championship.' He licked his finger and stroked his moustache flat.

'Mmmm,' I muttered. 'Gotta go.'

This was a disaster. Not only had I mysteriously qualified for a competition involving über-brainy people, but now everyone expected me to be able to do their homework for them and win the competition so we could have a party.

My mind raced with all the things that were going to happen when I scored zero at the championship.

- Mr Biggend would have a nervous breakdown.
- Mr Pitdown would be triumphant that he had been proved right.
- Everyone at school would hate me because Mr Biggend would cancel the party and reinstate Maths Day instead.

In other words, I was doomed.

It wasn't the National Brainiac Championship.

It was the National Humiliation Factor – with a very large H.

The only thing I was going to be winner of was *The H-Factor* and I wasn't looking forward to it.

7

Damage

Limitation

Jessie was putting her key in the front door when I got home. She totally ignored me and slammed the door in my face, leaving me outside.

Dober-Mum won't let me have my own key until I'm in senior school. Jessie knows this but really enjoys leaving me on the pavement like a pile of neglected dog poo.

Being locked out of my home by my own family was bad enough but when they heard the Kendal name being linked with the score of ZERO at the stupid championship, my family and their brains were going to completely disown me.

I'd be locked out for ever.

I headbutted the doorbell a few times and it must have woken up a few brain cells because I realised I could reduce the humiliation factor by NOT telling my family about the Brainiac Championship.

'I'm cooking tea,' Mum said when she let me in. 'What happened at school today?'

'Nothing,' I said as usual. Mum expected nothing different.

'Ticker!' Timmy said and pointed to his chest. 'Ticker, Dan-Dan.'

I knelt down to see the round purple sticker he was pointing at.

'Timmy got his first sticker at nursery,' Mum said. 'You're such a clever boy, aren't you?' Mum picked Timmy up and swung him round. 'That reminds me.' Mum put Timmy down. 'This letter arrived for you, Jess.' Mum thrust an envelope into Jessie's hands.

I think Mum already knew what was inside because instead of acting like Dober-Mum she was jumping up and down with her tongue hanging out like Dober-Puppy-About-To-Be-Fed.

'Ooh!' Jessie squealed. 'My tap-dancing results. How do you think I did?'

'Doesn't matter as long as you did your best.'

Mum always says that, but I've seen the disappointment on her face enough times when she opens my school report to know she doesn't mean it.

'I got distinction!' Jessie screamed.

'Well done! That's my girl!' Mum threw her arms around Jessie. 'I'm so proud of you.'

'Well done, Jessie.' Those were the words I was supposed to say but my über-successful sister didn't hear them because I didn't move my mouth or tongue. It didn't matter. She was squealing so much she wouldn't have heard me anyway.

'We're going to have to get an extension at this rate.' Mum looked over at the wall groaning with everyone's certificates and commendations.

She calls it the Shrine of Achievement. We each have our own section.

I got the Duckling1 certificate for turning up at swimming lessons when I was three and the driving licence from Legoland that they give to everyone who pays to have a go in their driving school. That was it. No real achievements in ten years.

'I'm going to make a special chart for you, Timmy, so you can add your stickers to it.'

'Hello, everyone.' Dad came through the front door with a huge smile on his face. 'Have I got news for you!'

The holiday to the States! I'd forgotten all about it. Hooray! Some good news that didn't involve a

member of my family showing off how brilliant they were. I didn't care about the stupid brainiac competition or the empty space on the Shrine of Achievement. We were going to Disneyworld, Universal Studios and SeaWorld!

'Wait for it.' Dad paused in a fake dramatic way before taking a piece of paper out of his jacket and slapping it on the Shrine of Achievement. 'I've been approached about a new job. A promotion!'

There wasn't space on the wall for more of Dad's brilliance. He already had two degrees, a PhD, an MSc and a zillion diplomas. He even had a certificate from his dental hygienist saying he had perfectly clean teeth. And now he had a promotion because he was so amazing at work.

'Fantastic!' Mum and Jessie shouted at the same time and threw their arms around Dad for a group hug. Timmy pushed in between their knees and hugged Dad's legs. I didn't feel in the mood for a Kendal family group hug. I wanted to go on holiday.

'I love you!' Mum said and kissed Dad full on the lips.

I turned away. Snogging between a dad and a Dober-Mum is totally disgusting.

'Can I have a new phone if you get a pay rise?' Jessie said.

'You're definitely going to need one where we're going.' Dad grinned. 'The new job is in the USA! America here we come!'

8

Where?

The letters hung in the air like a ghostly helium balloon lost at the fair, something special but just out of reach.

'America?' Mum's voice cracked the frozen silence.

'It's going to be amazing,' Dad said. 'The university there will give us a big house, a car and everything we need. You always wanted to go to America, Liz, and now's your chance.' Dad pulled Mum in for a big hug. 'Since you sent me on that fear of flying course, I realised I've been missing out on the world. We all have. So when I saw this opportunity, I applied. They've been in touch to arrange an interview because they want ME and both my brains.' Dad picked up his plastic brain with one hand and tapped his head with the other.

Mum didn't say much. I think she had a speck of dust in her eye or something because she kept dabbing it with a tissue.

'Fantastic!' Jessie said. 'I'm going to apply for the New York School of Performing Arts.' And then she started singing from the dumb musical she took part in last summer. She sidestepped/danced across the kitchen, throwing her arms in the air.

'That's not going to work, Jessie,' Dad said. 'We're not moving to New York. We're moving to Albuquerque.'

'Alber-where?' Jessie spluttered.

'Albuquerque, New Mexico,' Dad said with a dopey grin on his face.

'Mexico?' Jessie shrieked. 'I'm not moving to Mexico.'

'*New* Mexico, USA,' Dad said.

'Well, I'm NOT moving to Alberquirckly!'

'What do you think, Dan?' Dad must have suddenly remembered Jessie wasn't the only child who could contribute to the conversation.

I was thinking, *I've got it wrong again*. There was no US holiday. There was only some place far, far away with a weird name. It wasn't that long ago when I was thinking of leaving home and moving to a planet on the other side of the universe. I'd decided against it in the end. Right now, Albu-whatsit sounded just as far off.

'Dunno,' I said.

'A change might do you good,' Dad said. 'New school. New regime. You might do better in an American school.'

'What do you mean?' I said.

'Dad's saying you're thick, Peabrain,' Jessie said.

'I'm not a peabrain!' I said. I knew my brain was bigger than a pea because I couldn't hear it rattling around inside my head. But it was a good word to add to the NOT-brainiac word list.

'Yes, you are,' Jessie said.

'That's enough, Jessie,' Mum said. 'You are not a peabrain, Daniel. But maybe you could do better sometimes.'

'You're wrong!' I said. I was fed up with my family thinking I was stupid. I wasn't. I didn't have any posh certificates or letters after my name and I

was only trying hard to seem stupid so I could beat Freddo at something.

Before I knew what was happening, my brain cells fused together and created some words that jumped out of my mouth without me doing anything. 'I have been selected to represent the school in the National Brainiac Championship. I even beat Gordon. I got one hundred per cent in the test.'

'Really?' Mum said.

'That's fantastic, Dan.'

Dad looked at Mum. Mum looked at Dad. I knew what they were thinking.

'I'm really proud of you,' Dad said.

'That's amazing. Well done, Daniel.' Mum kissed the top of my head.

'What's the prize?' Jessie said. Her random mood generator was flickering.

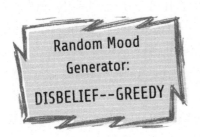

Random Mood
Generator:
DISBELIEF--GREEDY

'A shield with my name on it,' I said.

'Is that all? Do they give you a sword to go with the shield? I need one to murder you with.'

'That's enough, Jessie. Rob, you're going to have to fix a shelf on the Shrine of Achievement so we can display Dan's Brainiac shield.'

'I haven't won yet!'

I knew this would happen. I shouldn't have mentioned the competition. Mum was so pleased she turned into Dober-Puppy-Being-Fed-Treats. She was going to be SOOOO disappointed.

'I'm not interested in some rubbish shield.

I haven't finished talking about Alberquickly yet.' Jessie pushed me aside. 'I don't want to go. I don't want to leave my friends.'

'I've got friends too,' I said.

'You'll make new friends,' Dad said.

Me? Who was he kidding? I only had two friends, even if neither of them was talking to me right now.

'If I had friends like yours, I'd be begging Mum and Dad to take me away,' Jessie said. 'My friends are totally different. They are my life.'

'I thought One Dimension were your life,' I said.

A real brainiac would not have mentioned One Dimension at that moment.

'Arghh!' Jessie screamed.' I can't move to America. I'll miss the One Dimension European tour next year. I'M NOT GOING!'

Jessie was right. I was a peabrain.

I left her arguing with Mum and Dad and went upstairs. I didn't know what was going to be worse. Coming last in front of my friends at *The H-Factor* or leaving my friends (if they forgave me) to move abroad with my family.

Where was Alber-whatsit? I pulled out the atlas and flicked through the pages. New Mexico was at

the bottom of the map of the USA, north of Mexico. Slap bang in the middle of the state was a place called Albuquerque.

I still had my finger on the map when Jessie stormed into my room.

'This is ALL your fault!'

'But –'

Her eyes zoomed in on the spot I was pointing to on the map.

'Where is this place? Near Timbuktu?'

Jessie grabbed the atlas out of my hands.

'I'm not living in a place with two "q"s in the name. That's not normal.'

'It's got three "u"s too,' I said.

'Listen to me, little brother.' Jessie shoved the atlas under my chin, nearly choking me. 'I am not moving to somewhere in the middle of nowhere with an unpronounceable, impossible-to-spell name. Dad only thinks we need to move because you are such a stupid dumbo nitwit' – note to self: add *dumbo* and *nitwit* to the list – 'and have dodgy friends.'

'That's not true. He's got a new job over there.'

'Ha! That's what he said but the moment you mentioned the stupid brainiac thing, moving to America went clean out of his head. You HAVE to win that moronic competition to prove you're not as thick as Dad thinks you are, so we don't have to move.'

She hit me round the head with the atlas and stormed out. I sat on my bed, the sound of my tiny peabrain rattling around inside my skull.

I didn't want to move to Albuquerque any more than she did, but it wasn't my fault that Dad wanted to move there, AND there was no way I was ever going to win that competition. We might as well start packing for America now.

9

The Problem

with Emigration

'Have you ever heard of Albuquerque?' I asked Freddo and Gordon at break time the next day.

'I do not want to speak about Albuquerque, New Mexico, 35°06'39"N, 106°36'36"W, population 555,000.' Gordon's laptop was open but for once he wasn't looking at the screen. His eyes were fixed firmly on me. 'I want to talk about the qualification test for the National Brainiac Championship.'

'Sorry,' I said. 'I don't know what happened.'

'You're a lying cheat!' Freddo said. 'I thought we were in a competition to come last, not try to be brainiacs!'

'I'm not a cheat,' I said. 'I really wanted to do

badly. I knew the *Star Trek* question, like you. And then after that I just guessed.'

'How did you guess Question Two – the value of pi?' Gordon started some weird preening routine I'd never seen before. First he smoothed his eyebrows, then he checked his hair wasn't sticking out above his ears and he ended by twitching his nose. He kept his eyes fixed on me the whole time.

'There wasn't a question on pies,' Freddo said.

'Wasn't Question Two about Egyptian burial chambers?' I said. 'I think there was a picture of the entrance to one anyway.'

'Question Two was about a close approximation of pi, Mr Kendal.' Gordon turned his laptop towards me. On the screen was the same image of the entrance to an Egyptian burial chamber.

'That is the greek letter pi.'

'How does that have a value?' I said.

'I like minced beef and onion pie but my bruv prefers chicken and mushroom. They're both two pounds fifty at our chippie,' Freddo said.

'Dober-Mum makes the best chicken pie ever,' I said. 'She makes it herself but I don't know how much it costs.'

'I like apple pie as well,' Freddo said. 'Those little individual ones that come in a six pack are the best. Don't know how much they are, though. Mum buys them from the cash and carry.'

'Pi has nothing to do with food!' Gordon said. 'It is the relationship between a circle's radius and its circumference. It's approximately 3.14159265358979.'

'How do you know this stuff?' I said.

'I use a mnemonic – a way of remembering lists,' Gordon said. '*How I need a drink, alcoholic of course after the heavy lectures involving quantum mechanics.*'

Freddo yawned.

'I haven't got a clue what you are talking about,' I said.

'Take the number of letters from each word and it gives you the value of pi. "How" is three, "I" is 1, "need" is four, and so on.'

'I don't know how to spell quantum or mechanics,' I said.

'You can also express pi as a fraction, Mr Kendal,' Gordon droned on. He was clearly bored.

'I've never understood fractions,' Freddo said.

'Nah,' I agreed. 'They fry my brain.'

'The easiest one to remember is twenty-two over seven,' Gordon said.

'How do you remember that?' I said.

Gordon shrugged.

Freddo grabbed the pad off Gordon and squiggled something else on it. 'Two little ducks over the lucky number seven,' he said.

'Nice one,' I said. 'Ask me the question again.'

'What is the value of pie?' Freddo said.

'Twenty-two over seven,' I said and looked over to Gordon for confirmation.

'Correct,' he said. 'But Mr Biggend said you scored one hundred per cent in the test. How did you score full marks if you didn't know the value of pi?'

'No idea,' I said. 'I didn't even put my name on the paper.'

Gordon scowled slightly and raised his hand in the air, his finger pointing at the ceiling. 'Neither did I.' A pink glow crept over his cheeks. 'I failed to follow the first instruction. I corrected my error after everyone had left the classroom.'

'What are you saying?' Freddo said.

'I told Mr Pitdown and he allowed me to write my name on my paper afterwards.'

'Your paper or Dan's?' Freddo said, nodding his head in my direction.

Gordon closed his eyes for a moment. His eyelids flickered slightly. I think he was trying to remember what happened. His eyelids snapped open and he looked at me. Only his eyes had been transformed from the usual Geeky too-close-together eyes to a pair of demonic bulging eyeballs.

When Gordon doesn't get his own way his eyeballs turn über. Eyeballs are mainly white with bright red veins squiggling all over them. Only you can't see that bit because normally it's hidden in the eye socket. When Gordon gets annoyed his eyeballs bulge out of their sockets so far they nearly touch his glasses.

'My name may have ended up on your paper,' Gordon said in a robotic voice.

'Only if you put it there,' I said.

'An error may have occurred,' Gordon said.

'Yeah! A fatal error!' Freddo said. 'Gordon's name ended up on your paper, so Mr Biggend must have thought the brilliant, one hundred per cent correct test paper with no name was yours, Dan! You are going to do SO badly in the Brainiac Championship.'

'I know.' I looked up at the sky, willing a bolt of lightning to take me out there and then. This was the worst mess I'd ever been in.

'Awesome!' Freddo said.

I didn't feel awesome. Pretending to be stupid with Freddo was one thing. Actually looking stupid in public was something else.

'You did not win the quiz,' Gordon said. 'I did.'

He was right, but I couldn't back out now. Somehow the Brainiac Championship/*The H-Factor* had got all muddled up with moving/not moving to America. If there was any chance of staying here with my friends, I was going to have to enter the competition. Gordon couldn't interfere.

'Not according to Mr Biggend,' I said.

Gordon the Demon's shoulders heaved and his eyes went all glassy. Gordon doesn't cry because he doesn't like to get tears on his clothes and he's allergic to snot. He sniffed loudly and pulled his wet eyeballs back into his skull.

'You are correct.' He let out a big sigh and looked down at his laptop screen again. 'The headmaster did announce you as the winner in front of the whole of Year 6. I have to abide by his decision.'

'Thanks, Gordon. Mum and Dad got totally carried away and think I'm going to win, and Jessie wants me to win so we don't have to move to Albuquerque.'

'What is this Alber-thing?' Freddo said as he frowned into the packet in his hand. 'Open wide!' Freddo lobbed a Hula Hoop at me. I ducked forward and caught it in my mouth.

Crunch!

'Albuquerque,' I said as I munched. 'In the USA.

Dad's been offered a job there. We might be moving. Will you come and visit?'

'No. I will not,' Gordon said. 'There are CCTV cameras everywhere at airports. The latest research suggests that CCTV degrades the brain. I am now avoiding CCTV as a matter of principle. I do not do video cameras. Therefore I do not do airports.'

'What a load of rubbish!' Freddo said. 'If cameras sucked out our brains, we'd all be fathead zombies.'

Add *fathead* to the list.

'Correct.' Gordon stared at Freddo for a couple of seconds, then turned his back on him. 'In addition, air travel is guaranteed to make you ill. Too many germs. No open windows. AND you have a full body search and your fingerprints taken with black ink when you enter the USA.' Gordon shivered.

'Do you want to go to the States, Dan?' Freddo crumpled up the Hula-Hoop bag and shoved it in his back pocket.

'For a holiday, yes,' I said. 'But I don't want to live there.'

'Emigration is a very big decision,' Gordon said.

'I thought emigration was what birds do when they fly south in the winter,' I said.

'That's migration. Emigration is humans moving to another country to live,' Gordon said. 'For ever.'

F O R   E V E R is a long time.

I might start talking in an American accent and calling the pavement the sidewalk and other stuff like that. And I'd probably have to join the basketball team because I am so tall. But I don't know how to play basketball, so I'd be useless and everyone would laugh at me.

I'd have no friends in America. For ever.

'I don't want to emigrate,' I said and my voice sounded all wobbly.

'I'll come and visit if you do,' Freddo said and held up his hand for a high five. 'The CCTV cameras can't do much more to my brain.'

'I am sorry that we will no longer be friends when you emigrate,' Gordon said.

'You can talk on Facebook,' Freddo said.

'We can't have a Facebook account until we are thirteen,' Gordon said.

'You can tell Facebook you're thirteen,' Freddo said. 'It's a computer program. It won't know.'

Gordon's eyebrows disappeared under his fringe. In horror, I expect. There was no way he would lie

about his age.

'You could Skype,' I said hurriedly. I didn't want to lose touch completely. They were the only friends I was ever going to have. I couldn't imagine anyone in America liking me.

'No cameras.' Gordon waggled his ultra clean finger in front of my face.

'Email, then,' I said.

Freddo and Gordon shrugged.

It was clear they were never going to stay in touch if I moved away.

'I don't want to go. Neither does Jessie. She thinks it's possible to make Dad change his mind.'

'How?' Freddo said.

'By winning the National Brainiac Championship. Will you help me?'

10

How to Become
a Brainiac

I think it's fair to say Freddo and Gordon didn't think it very likely I could ever become the National Brainiac Champion.

'I should be entering the competition,' Gordon said. 'You don't even know how to spell Albuquerque.'

'You can teach me,' I said. 'I've got to win.' Jessie's random mood generator was revving up for my failure, and I was in her sights.

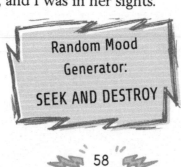

Random Mood
Generator:

SEEK AND DESTROY

'I want my name on the shield,' Gordon said. Then he did his eyebrow-stroking routine again. Gordon has loads of weird habits. This one might have indicated he was stressed.

'No problem,' I said. 'I'll tell them I want the name of my chief coach, Gordon Franks, on the shield instead of my own as I couldn't have done it without you.'

'You'll have to win first,' Freddo said.

I ignored him.

'Okay,' Gordon said as he opened his briefcase and took out a pair of black leather gloves. He pulled them on before holding out his hand to shake mine.

'Look, mate, I don't mean to be rude but . . .' Freddo pulled me next to Gordon. 'Your head is not exactly Geek size.'

'Head size doesn't matter when it comes to intelligence,' I said. 'That's what Dad says, anyway. And he is a brain expert.'

'Really?' Freddo crossed his arms and looked at me in a quizzical way. 'So you think it's a coincidence that Gordon has the biggest head out of the three of us and he is the brainiest?'

Gordon put his gloves away and took a

dressmaker's tape measure out of his briefcase. He wrapped it round his head.

'61.24 centimetres,' he said as he tapped some numbers into his laptop.

Freddo peered over his shoulder. 'Are you keeping track of the size of your head?'

'I am,' Gordon said. 'Look.'

'Since last year I have been eating a brain-boosting diet and, as you can see, the circumference of my head has grown five per cent. I also scored one hundred per cent in Mr Biggend's brainiac test. Last year I only scored ninety-six per cent.'

'We didn't do the test last year,' Freddo said.

'I did. Mr Pitdown put me in for it even though I was in Year 5.' Gordon blinked once.

'You didn't win?'

'No. I got one question wrong, but I have been eating loads of brain-boosting spirulina pondweed since then,' Gordon said. 'It's bright green.'

'Radioactive pondweed!' I said. 'No, thanks!'

'It is organic and an important part of this diet plan – which is going to be essential if you really wish to increase the capacity of your brain in only two weeks.'

'Anything else?' I said, even though I was feeling sick already.

'I have prepared a comprehensive diet and study regime.' Gordon handed Freddo the tape measure.

'We can record the size of Mr Kendal's brain to monitor if it is working.'

Freddo measured my head.

56.1 centimetres.

'8.39% less than mine,' said Gordon.

I was going to have to eat a lot of pondweed.

11

A Brainiac's
Diet

There was no way I was going to be able to eat all the things on Gordon's list.

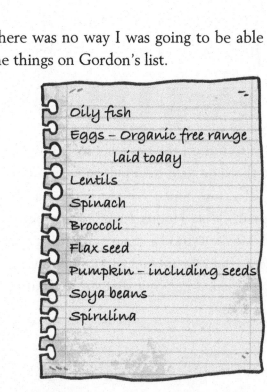

Oily fish

Eggs – Organic free range
    laid today

Lentils

Spinach

Broccoli

Flax seed

Pumpkin – including seeds

Soya beans

Spirulina

Even the snack list looked terrifyingly healthy.

Snacks:
Walnuts
Dried nori seaweed
Kale crisps

I decided to put off the new diet for a few days. I scrunched the food list into a ball and slam-dunked it into a litter bin. Since Freddo and I had been practising with Hula Hoops, I was getting better at basketball. Maybe I stood a chance of getting picked for the team when we moved to Albuquerque.

'Gordon emailed me your diet sheet,' Mum said when I got home.

'I was thinking of giving the brainiac food a miss,' I said.

'You can't do that. I've been to the health food shop and spent a fortune. They've got loads of stuff I've never heard of before. Look at this.'

'Rabbit droppings?' I said.

'Goji berries. Open wide.' She threw a berry at me and like an idiot I caught it in my mouth. As my teeth snapped on the dried fruit I realised my mistake. Instead of a light, crispy potato snack I got . . .

. . . rabbit droppings.

Having seen Freddo and Rooners in action the

day before, I knew exactly what to do.

'Next time you might as well get the rabbit to poop directly into the bin,' I said. 'Cut out the middle man.'

'Can't be that bad.' Mum put a goji berry into her mouth.

Not bad.

Quite nice.

Sort of tangy.

Lovely.

Totallly delicious.

Yuk!

'Maybe they need to be cooked,' she said, a goji-berry-sized bump bulging at her cheek. 'Soften them up a bit.'

There is a name for softened rabbit's droppings. It is bunny diarrhoea.

I wasn't eating it.

The windows rattled in their frames as the front door slammed shut. Jessie was home.

'SUP?' she said. Jessie texts so often she even speaks in text sometimes. It's something in the way she says it. And her text messages are always in capitals.

'Chicken pie, sweetcorn and mashed potato for tea,' Mum said.

'GUD. GTG.' She disappeared into the sitting room and the computer keyboard started clattering.

I never get a chance to go on the computer after school. Not only do I need more pocket money I also need a laptop of my own. Mum and Dad obviously think I'm too stupid to use a computer. But I'd prove them wrong if they bought me one.

'Teatime,' Mum yelled to anyone who was listening. 'Lay the table.'

I don't mind helping lay the table when it's chicken pie for tea. Mum always gives me a bigger portion if I'm helpful. But today was different.

'So pleased you're taking this brain training seriously,' Dad said as he sat down to eat. 'Sardines are very good for you.'

I shoved my knife into the belly of the weird lump on my plate and flipped it open.

'Argh!' I jumped up and hid behind the door. 'A fossilised tapeworm!'

Dad peered into the guts of my sardine.

'That is the bone. Mash it up with the fish. It's full of calcium.'

'This is scrummy, Mum.' Jessie lifted her fork loaded with crispy pastry and dripping with gravy and wafted it across the table at me.

My mouth filled with hungry saliva.

'Can I have chicken pie instead?' I said.

'Sorry. There's none left,' said Mum.

Every member of my family pulled their plates closer to them. Even Timmy was shovelling food in with a spoon like there was no tomorrow. He'd spread loads of it round his face, though. I was so hungry I nearly leapt across the table and licked it off.

'Shall we learn some facts while we're here?' Dad said. 'Multi-sensory learning is very important. Associate certain facts with certain tastes and you'll be able to recall them more easily. What's twelve squared?'

I didn't know what squared meant.

'Mmrujchgiahg mmrummhfgt,' Jessie said, her mouth stuffed full of my favourite meal.

'Don't talk with your mouth full,' Mum said.

'Come on, Dan. It's an easy question,' Dad said.

The only way I could avoid answering was to stuff my face with brain food. I stabbed the green thing covered in cat sick next to the sardine and shoved it in my mouth.

'Twelve squared means twelve times itself – and the answer is 144,' Dad said.

I closed my eyes and chewed on the disgustingness in my mouth. I didn't care if twelve squared was 144. I wanted to eat chicken pie, but I was scheduled to eat nothing but brain enhancing muck for another two weeks.

Mum had stuck the email from Gordon with my meal plans on the fridge door.

Weetabix – yes, with fried egg – no. After tea I took out a pen and scribbled out the weird addition.

I was going to have to have a word with Gordon about this diet. At this rate I was going to die of starvation long before the Brainiac Championship.

12

Stretch

That Brain

All that brain food was doing weird things to my insides. If Freddo challenged me to a farting competition he'd lose for the first time ever. And I was worried it would be more than just gas coming out. If I carried on eating like this I ran a serious risk of embarrassing myself in my trousers. Even Timmy didn't do that any more.

'I'm giving up on the diet,' I told Freddo and Gordon at break time the next day.

'Do you want to become National Brainiac Champion?' Gordon said.

'Yes,' I said, 'but your food is doing strnge things to me and the gas has to get out somehow. Either

I fart for England or the top of my head explodes.'

'Let me know when you're ready to blow,' Freddo said. 'I don't want to get brain splatter on my new trackies.'

'My head is pounding and all you are interested in is your clothes?' Sometimes Freddo is the most selfish best friend a NOT-brainiac could ever have.

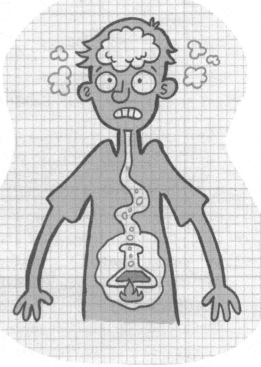

'You have a headache. Good.' Gordon looked up for a moment, straightened his eyebrows and blinked a couple of times before he looked back at his laptop. 'Your brain is growing but your skull is not big enough to accommodate the additional brain cells.'

'So my growing brain is trying to smash its way out?' This was getting dangerous. I was too young to die.

'I suggest we act quickly to increase the size of the skull as a precaution,' Gordon said in a bored tone.

'How?'

'Shall we reconvene at your premises at 16.30 hours?' Gordon said.

'Is that six o'clock or eight o'clock?' Freddo said.

'Half past four in the afternoon, Mr O'Connor. We will need a cycle helmet.'

'I've got one,' I said.

'And these.' Gordon handed a piece of paper to Freddo.

'No problemo,' Freddo said.

'What's on the list?' I said but Freddo had already gone. Anyway, I didn't care what Gordon did to me as long as my headache and terrible stomach ache disappeared and I didn't embarrass myself in my trousers.

* * *

Later on, Gordon laid out the components on my bedroom floor.

I take it back about Freddo being selfish. His dad has a zillion lock-up garages stuffed full of anything he might be able to sell on his market stall. He lets Freddo help himself to whatever he wants and Freddo gives the stuff to me and Gordon without question.

Freddo's dad did not stock protective clothing on any of his market stalls and Gordon's hazmat suit must have been lost in the post.

Gordon may be my second best friend but he still thinks I might contaminate him.

'Do you still have the false vampire teeth from Halloween?' Gordon asked, his voice muffled by the green mask over his face.

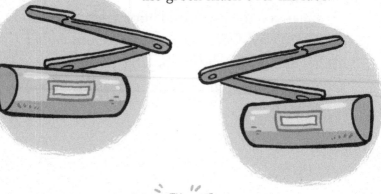

'Somewhere,' I said and indicated the mass of stuff crammed under the chair in the corner of my room.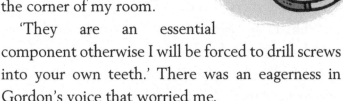

'They are an essential component otherwise I will be forced to drill screws into your own teeth.' There was an eagerness in Gordon's voice that worried me.

'I'll find them . . . Somehow. Can I borrow this?' I picked up the head torch and slipped the elastic over my head. 'I'm going in.' I dropped to my hands and knees and shone the torch into the darkness under the chair.

'Pull me out by the ankles if I stop moving,' I said to Freddo.

I could see old *Beanos*, odd socks, a zillion nerf gun bullets. A dinosaur that belonged to Timmy. And right at the back I found the plastic teeth.

Gordon eyed them suspiciously when I showed them to him.

'Sterilisation required,' he said, taking a step back.

'You're double gloved,' I said.

'These gloves protect against E. coli and salmonella, not the sort of wildlife that might be living in the forgotten corners of your bedroom.'

'Shh! Dober-Mum might hear you. She'll make me clean up and then we'll have to stop what we are doing. I tell you, my head is about to explode!' I pulled off the head torch, but it didn't make any difference.

'Clean your teeth.' Gordon opened the bedroom door and pointed to the bathroom.

I don't like being bossed around by Gordon's hang-ups but I didn't fancy flossing with spider's web so I gave the teeth a rinse in the bathroom sink before putting them in my mouth.

Gordon shoved the cycle helmet on my head and wound the elastic head band from my head torch over it and under my jaw, to keep it on my head.

'WWWWWWWWWWWWWW,' I said. Or at least I tried to say it, only the elastic was so tight I couldn't actually open my mouth.

Gordon ignored me. He took one of the door closers and jammed it into the air holes in my helmet.

'Suits you, Dan,' Freddo snorted.

Gordon attached an elastic band to the other end

of the door closers and pulled them in front of my face.

'Open wide,' he said.

'WWWWWWWWWW,' I said.

He prised my lips open with a pencil and hooked the elastic bands onto my vampire fangs.

It felt like the bones in my skull were being prised apart.

'You'll need to wear it constantly for the next two weeks to allow the skull to stretch,' Gordon said as he sprayed his gloved fingers with disinfectant.

'WWWWWWWWWWWWWW,' I said. My head ached even more now, but I had to give it a go if it meant I stood a chance at winning the Brainiac Championship.

'What happens if I do this?' Freddo said as he twanged my elastic.

'WWWWWWWWWWWWWWW,' I said.

'Awesome!' Freddo laughed. 'They are going to love you at school.'

He was supposed to be my first best friend but he was laughing at me.

'For it to be effective, you should wear it as much as possible. Twelve hours a day should be enough,' Gordon said. 'Can you walk?'

Have you ever tried walking with two industrial-strength spring-loaded door-closing mechanisms strapped to your head? It was like wearing a sleeping, but deadly, octopus for a hat. I had to keep my movements steady or Gordon's contraption woke up and tried to rip my head off. I took tiny footsteps, keeping my eyes front at all times, which was really difficult when all I could hear was Freddo rolling about on the floor, howling like a mad sheepdog.

I stood at the top of the stairs wondering how I was going to make it down alive.

'If you are going to increase your skull size safely, you must stay vertical at all times,' Gordon the Tyrant said.

Thanks, mate, I thought. But I didn't dare open my mouth in case he'd rigged his contraption to go bonkers if I complained.

I was still working up the courage to take my first step when Jessie came charging up the stairs with a boy I'd never seen before.

'What are you up to, Peabrain?' Jessie screeched.

I couldn't answer.

'Bozo!' Jessie said to her (boy)friend. 'LOL!'

They both cracked up. The boy sounded like a

donkey. Jessie sounded more like a pig. The whole farmyard was laughing at me.

Jessie grabbed the boy's hand and dragged him into her bedroom. 'Do not disturb, Numbskull. Yeah?' She slammed the door to her room.

Bozo. Numbskull. Two more words for the list.

I tried to take a step downstairs but the movement sent the spring-loaded door-closers mental. They swung out in opposite directions and tried to turn my head inside out, teeth first.

'WAWAWAWAAA!' Screaming made the pain worse.

I ripped off the rubber bands and spat my fake teeth out onto the carpet.

I wasn't stupid enough to ever dare disturb Jessie but I really was a bozo numbskull if I let Gordon pull my head apart.

13

Hello,

America

Gordon was annoyed with me for refusing to complete his diet and brain-stretching plan, so he ignored me all the next day at school. I didn't care. I needed a total break from everything to do with brains and Mum had promised me burger and chips for tea and an evening in front of the television.

But when I got home, Jessie was in the hallway. Bright red face, eyes flashing neon blue and her gnashing teeth a zillion times scarier than my vampire teeth ever were.

'Do something!' she shouted. 'Do something now!'

Jessie went mental so often it was impossible to know if there was a genuine crisis.

'Look!' Jessie pointed to a sign on the sitting room door.

DO NOT DISTURB!
Online interview
with America

'Dad's on Skype with an American. They're laughing and joking! The conversation is going TOO well. You need to get in there to stop him or the guy will offer him the job.'

'But . . .' What could I do?

Jessie opened the door and pushed me into the sitting room.

Dad was sitting in front of the computer. On the screen was a red-faced man wearing a baseball cap. His flabby neck oozed out of the collar of his shirt.

'See you've got company there, Rob. Wanna introduce us?'

'This is my son, Daniel,' Dad said in a sad attempt at an American accent. He pulled me into the range of the webcam and draped his arm over my shoulders. 'Say hi to Mr Bragman.'

'Howdy, Danny Boy.' Mr Bragman held out his hand as if to shake my hand, only there were two computer screens, the whole Atlantic and various bits of continent in the way so I couldn't actually touch him. 'Nice knowing ya. Ya looking forward to moving out here to the land of the free?'

'Yeah,' I muttered. I couldn't exactly say anything else now that I was part of Dad's job interview.

'What's your favourite subject at school?'

'Break time,' I said.

'Break? D'you mean recess?' he said. 'That's hilarious.' When he laughed the buttons strained on his shirt. 'Don't you worry, we have plenty of recess over here. Also social studies, history, math-e-matics. All the university faculty's kids go to Albuquerque High. They're all high achievers like you and your pa.'

Oh no! Even Dad's new boss thought I was a brainiac. I hoped Dad hadn't told him about the competition.

'Dan's really looking forward to it, aren't you,

Dan?' Dad thumped me on the back.

'Sure thing,' I said, trying to sound enthusiastic.

'Me and your pa have a few more things to discuss. Nice to meet ya, Danny Boy, and I look forward to meeting you in person real soon.'

'Bye, Mr Bragman.'

'Call me BW. Short for Big Willie. Everyone else does.' He laughed and his belly jiggled under his shirt. 'Can't wait to welcome you into the University of Albuquerque family, Danny Boy.'

I edged backwards out of the camera shot. Dad gave me the thumbs up and then sat down again to continue his conversation with Big Willie Bragman. If Dad gets the job, I'm going to have to lie to Freddo and Gordon about Dad's new boss's name.

In the kitchen Mum and Jessie were stuffing themselves with an über-sized box of chocolates.

'I'm pleased you're giving up the brainiac diet,' Mum said. 'I can always sprinkle a few flax seeds on top of your burger to boost your Omega 3.'

'Don't bother,' I said. 'I think it's too late.'

'How about a chocolate? I bought them to cheer myself up.'

There were only two left. Mum usually only

binged on chocolate when she'd had a row with Dad. But I hadn't heard them arguing for ages.

She unwrapped the chocolate and threw it for me to catch in my mouth exactly like Freddo would have done. My teeth crushed the chocolate shell and the soft centre squidged out across my taste buds. It was the most delicious thing I'd ever eaten. I don't know why anyone would prefer to eat goji berries.

Dad rushed into the kitchen, a huge grin across his face.

'The job is mine if I want it.' He punched the air.

'Congratulations, Rob!' Mum croaked as if she had a chocolate stuck in her throat.

'I thought you were going to fix it so Dad didn't get the job,' Jessie hissed in my ear as she grabbed my wrist and twisted my arm up my back.

'Jessie, you should have come in and spoken to Willie,' Dad said.

'Willie?' Jess spluttered.

'He's big,' I muttered.

'He's great, isn't he, Dan? I reckon your joke about break time clinched it.'

'You were making jokes with the enemy?' Jessie yanked my hand harder. I squealed.

'I think BW was really impressed with you, Dan,' Dad said.

Jessie kicked my leg.

Mum must have realised what Jessie was doing to me because the corner of her left eye twitched constantly, which only happens when she's stressed. But for some reason she didn't say anything.

Dad rattled on about all things America. High school, back yards, baseball, dimes and quarters.

'It's my dream job!' He grabbed the peppermill from the table, jumped up onto the table and started singing some old song asking if this was the real life or just fantasy.

It seemed all too real to me.

'Get down, Rob,' Mum said as she tried to stop Timmy climbing out of his high chair.

'P-lease!' Jessie said and hid her face in her hands.

'If I can't sing "Bohemian Rhapsody" on the day I'm offered the biggest job of my life, when can I sing it?'

'Never,' Jessie said.

'Come on, Dan, join in with me.' He stomped his socked foot on the table and sang again.

'You need to know this stuff,' Dad said. 'The

opening lines of "Bohemian Rhapsody" might be a question at the quiz. It might make the difference between winning and losing the Brainiac Championship.'

'They are more likely to ask about things that are up to date,' I said. 'You know – NOW.'

'Yeah, like the names of the members of One Dimension,' Jessie said. 'They are very now.'

I groaned. Everyone in our house knew the names of the members of One Dimension. Even Timmy.

'"Boh Rap" is a classic,' Dad said.

'*Classic* means *old*,' I said. 'An old song for old people.'

'For dead people,' Jessie said.

'I am not dead,' Dad said.

'Freddy Mercury is,' Mum said.

My head started spinning. Who was Freddy Mercury? I didn't need my poor brain being clogged up with Mum and Dad's facts about ancient music and dead people.

'I'm so looking forward to coming to see you at the quiz,' Dad said as he climbed down from the chair.

'Parents aren't allowed,' I said.

'Yes, they are.' Mum reached over and picked up a piece of paper. 'Mr Biggend wrote asking how many tickets we wanted. Do you want to come, Jessie?'

'No!' I shouted.

Mum ignored me.

'Do I get a day off school?' Jessie said.

'I guess so,' Mum said. 'It's midweek.'

'I'll come then,' Jessie said.

'We'll all be there to support you, Dan.' Dad patted me on the back.

'I don't want—' I spluttered.

'What does Dan get if he wins?' Jessie said.

'Anything he wants,' Dad said.

Random Mood
Generator:

BRIGHT IDEA

'Hear that, Dan?' She nudged me. 'ANYTHING you want. You can ask Dad for ANYTHING at all.'

I know what she wanted. Jessie wanted me to use my wild card on asking NOT to go to America. But what about me? What was I going to get out of this whole stupid Brainiac thing? I wanted a laptop.

Do you think, if by some miracle I win, Dad will give up on America AND buy me a laptop?

14

Never Give Up,
Never Surrender

Gordon was particularly annoyed when he realised I hadn't even tried spirulina.

'I'm sorry, Gordon,' I said. 'I want to win the Brainiac competition, so I don't look a total idiot. But I don't want to look a total idiot while I am preparing for the competition either. And I can't eat pondweed. I'm not a frog.'

'Frogs don't eat pondweed. They are carnivorous. They typically eat flies and bugs. Let's see if there has been any change to your head's circumference.' Gordon took his tape measure out of his briefcase and handed it to Freddo who wrapped it round my head.

'55.7 centimetres,' Freddo read out.

'Are you sure?' Gordon looked puzzled as he consulted his spreadsheet.

Freddo measured my head again.

'Yeah,' he said.

'Your head has shrunk.' Gordon snapped shut his laptop.

'I'm never going to win. Jessie is right. I am a bozo.'

'I don't know what you're worried about,' Freddo said. 'You are going to be famous for getting the lowest score ever on a national competition. That's awesome.'

'Don't you get it, Freddo? I don't exactly want to be a brainiac, but I'm fed up of people thinking I'm stupid. Because I am not.'

'Are you sure about that?' Freddo asked.

'Yes! I have a brain!' I wanted to punch him. Didn't Freddo realise being a NOT-brainiac was so yesterday. 'And I need to fill my brain with facts.'

'I agree,' Gordon said. 'Which is why I prepared this for you.' Gordon handed me a slim leather case. 'Listen to it at bedtime, while you fall asleep. Keep it playing all night. When you wake up you'll remember it all.'

It was an iPhone. Not the very latest model, but

it didn't have a scratch on it. I guess it was one of Gordon's old phones but he didn't even ask me to wash my hands before I touched it.

'Give it here.' Freddo tried to snatch it out of my hand. 'Has it got any good apps?'

'I'll give it a go.' I pulled it away from Freddo's greasy grasp. 'Thanks, Gordon.'

Gordon is many things: a geek, a neat freak, a total brainiac. But he is also a very good friend. Maybe that is the difference between brainiacs and everyone else. Brainiacs never give up.

I took the brain-training iPhone home. It was Mum's Zumba class night. She had prepared a sandwich tea as usual so I was able to sneak a plate of food upstairs. Hopefully, this would be a pain-free way to cram my brain.

I have the smallest room in the house but I have a loft bed, which makes it feel bigger. I love my loft bed. I feel in my own little world when I'm lying on it. My bed fits into the end of the room perfectly and the ceiling isn't far away so when I lie there it's like being in a box. And if I put my Halloween vampire outfit on, I feel like I'm in a coffin. I love it.

I was going to need a real coffin if we ended up moving to Albuquerque. Jessie would blame me and probably drive a stake through my heart even though I'd only dressed like Dracula once. When was Jessie going to realise IT WASN'T MY FAULT!

I plugged my headphones into Gordon's iPhone and lay back in my coffin bed to hear what was on it.

'What is the chemical symbol for hydrogen?' Gordon's voice said in my ear.

'I don't know,' I replied.

'H,' he answered.

'What is hydrogen?' I said but Gordon's voice wasn't listening to what I was saying.

'What is the chemical symbol for potassium?'

No, no, no! Another thing I'd never heard of.

'P?' I said.

'K,' Gordon answered.

How was I supposed to remember that?

'What is the chemical symbol for zirconium?'

'Shut up!' I shouted and prodded the shuffle button hoping to come up with a better question.

'What is the atomic number of platinum?'

I pressed shuffle again. This was hopeless. I'd never heard of chemical symbols or atomic numbers.

I didn't know anything.

Gordon's voice droned in my ears. All the questions sounded the same to me. My eyelids felt heavy.

'What is the atomic number of cadmium?'

I don't know.

'What is the chemical symbol for tin?'

I don't know.

'What is the atomic number of iodine?'

I don't know.

All I knew was that I knew nothing at all. I just hoped that Gordon was right and all these chemical symbols and atomic numbers would somehow take up residence in my brain and that in the morning I would know the answer to everything.

I was woken by a hockey stick jabbing me in the ribs. Jessie was at the other end and I'd guess by the way her mouth was moving, she was shouting. But all I could hear was Gordon saying, 'What is the chemical symbol for potassium?'

'I still don't know!' I shouted.

Jessie jabbed me with the stick again and Gordon said, 'K.'

'Okay, it's K! The chemical symbol for potassium

is K. Now shut up!' I pulled the headphones out of my ears and sat up in bed.

The problem with having a loft bed when you are very tall is that if you sit up too quickly, you smack your head on the ceiling.

'Do you know what time it is?' Jessie shouted.

'I don't know,' I said.

'Time for school,' she shouted and stormed out of the room.

My head spun in a weird way. It might have been the bang on my head or it might have been the overload of facts that Gordon had drilled into my brain all night. But at least I was already dressed.

'You okay, Dan?' Dad said.

'I don't know,' I said.

'How come you're wearing the same shirt as yesterday?' Mum said.

'I don't know,' I said.

I'm sure there were chemical facts slushing about in my head but I hadn't a clue what any of them were.

'Did you learn anything last night?' Gordon asked when I got to school.

'I don't know,' I said. It seemed to be the only

thing I was capable of saying this morning. My head was thumping now. Not with brain-food-induced gas this time. With despair.

'What is the chemical symbol for potassium?'

'He doesn't know it.' Freddo yawned. 'Nor do I. And what's more, I don't care. Can we do something else? Or I'm going out to play football.'

'Go then!' I shouted. A rampant Jacuzzi feeling bubbled up inside me. The water was so hot my face flushed red and all I wanted to do was jump out of the tub. Freddo was the last thing I needed right now. I was in this mess because of our stupid NOT-brainiac contest. A contest *he* came up with.

'I knew the chemical symbol for potassium this morning,' I said to Gordon. 'I can't remember what it is but I know it's not P.'

'The answer is K,' Gordon said.

Gordon was right, of course. He was always right. I was always wrong. And always would be. Someone turned the panicky Jacuzzi jets off inside my guts. I sat on the step and wrapped my head in my hands.

'I give up,' I said. 'I'm going to withdraw from the National Brainiac Championships. You can do it instead, Gordon.'

'No, I cannot,' Gordon said.

'Of course you can.' I looked up. 'You're the one who really got one hundred per cent in the test. You won't have to revise or anything. You'll get your name on the shield and everything. You are the true brainiac.'

'I might know the answers to the questions but I'm not going on the quiz,' Gordon said.

'Why not?' Freddo said.

Gordon pointed to a poster on the wall behind him.

'I don't do TV cameras. They are 6.78 times worse at degrading the brain than CCTV,' Gordon said.

'What?' The bubbling Jacuzzi was back. Only this time it was full of molten lava. I was being fried from the inside out. '*The H-Factor* will be on TV?'

'Nice one, Dan.' Freddo patted me on the back. 'You are going to get the lowest score ever on a quiz show on national television!'

Everyone I knew would be watching the show. They were ALL going to see what a TOTAL idiot I was. In fact, EVERYONE in the WHOLE WORLD would see it and they'd all be laughing at me.

'I can't do it,' I said to Freddo. 'I can't.' My tall NOT-brainiac body started shaking and big tears plopped onto the floor of the corridor. 'Help me, Freddo. Please!'

The thing with Freddo is that he tries to make out he's not really interested in my crazy schemes, but when it comes to the crunch – he delivers.

'It'll be okay,' he said. 'Gordon knows the answers. All we've got to do is work out a way of getting them to you.'

'What do you mean?' I wailed.

'We work out how to cheat,' Freddo said.

'I can't cheat,' I said.

'It won't be cheating if you get Gordon's name on that shield,' Freddo said. 'He'll go down in history as the winner of the National Brainiac Championship this year, not you.'

I wasn't so sure.

DANIEL KENDAL
THE CHEAT.

DANIEL KENDAL
THE LIAR.

DANIEL KENDAL
THE FAKE.

Maybe it was better to score zero and die of humiliation on national TV.

Once I was dead, Mum could put my urn of ashes on the new shelf on the Shrine of Achievement, and rename it the Shrine of Humiliation. I had plenty of things to add to that.

Humiliating Things That Have Happened to Me in My Life			
Age	What I Did	How Many People Saw	Humiliation Factor
3	Wet my pants while watching Jessie's school play	17	51
6	Mistook a Moshi Monster for a Pokémon character	6	36
7	Was mistaken for a girl when I dressed up as a pirate wearing a long black wig and bandana	11	77
8	Cried when I lost Dad in the supermarket	2	16
9	Scored an own goal in football because I didn't know which was our end	24	216

But I think answering zero on global TV channel would be worse than all of them put together. Someone was bound to post it on YouTube and it might go viral.

I was going to have to drag the humiliation factor around with me FOR EVER.

Everyone in my family would suffer.

Dad would be sacked by Big Willie Bragman of the University of Albuquerque for being the dad of a bozo.

The shame would send Dober-Mum so mad everyone would think she had rabies and she would have to be put down.

Jessie's donkey-laugh boyfriend would dump her.

Timmy's teachers would think he was as stupid as his big brother and only give him *Nice Try* stickers instead of *Good Work*.

I couldn't put my family through it.

I had to take part in that quiz and I had to win. And there was only one way I was going to do that.

I didn't like it but I had no choice.

I was going to have to cheat.

15

The Millionaire
Fraudster

'How do I do it?' I said to Freddo and Gordon when they came round to my house after school.

'That depends what "it" you are talking about?' Gordon looked up and waggled his eyebrows over the top of his glasses.

Freddo smirked.

I knew what they both were thinking and it was pathetic. We were supposed to be preparing for the most important event in my life and all they could think about was the 'IT' we had learned about in Year 6 Sex Ed last week. Rooners rolled about every time anyone said the word 'IT', but I really thought Gordon would think 'IT' far too messy for him.

'Are you leaving Team Brainiac to join the Football Gang?' I said.

'No!' Gordon straightened his eyebrows for the hundredth time that day. 'I don't think that would be a good idea.'

'Good, because I've got to win *The H-Factor* and the only way I'm going to do that is if . . .' I looked over my shoulder to see if anyone could overhear me. '. . . I C-H-E-A-T.'

'What are you talking about?' Freddo scowled. 'What's crate?'

'Not crate,' I hissed. Freddo was a natural NOT-brainiac. 'I spelled out CHEAT.'

'You're going to cheat!' Freddo's voice boomed out and echoed around my room.

'Shhh! I don't want my family to know! I don't want anyone to know.' Especially Mr Pitdown. I could see him smirking under his moustache right now.

'It's not a secret any more,' Gordon said. 'You've just told us.'

'Of course I told you!' I said. 'You're going to have to help me!'

Gordon's eyes roamed around his eye sockets for

a minute. I think it's a trait of all geniuses that they can't cheat.

'I don't want to be humiliated in public. You want your name on the Brainiac shield. Jessie wants me to stop Dad taking my family to Albuquerque for ever,' I said. 'Somehow I have to win.'

Worry lines wriggled across Gordon's forehead. He took extra care at smoothing his eyebrows, and checked his hair wasn't sticking out above his ears and twitched the end of his nose.

'Okay,' he said.

Gordon was the best second best friend you could have.

'How do we do it?' I asked.

'We break into the Brainiac HQ and steal the questions,' Freddo said.

'Mr Kendal,' Gordon said. 'I have to inform you that while I am prepared to help you win the competition, I am not prepared to break the law.'

'Me neither,' I said. 'Any other ideas?'

Freddo coughed suddenly, spraying me with crisp debris.

'Freddo!' I yelled and wiped cheese and onion crumbs off my face.

'That's the answer,' Freddo said. 'Coughing. That's what they did on *Who Wants to be a Millionaire?*. Check it out on YouTube.'

Gordon's hands sprinted across the keys of his laptop until I heard the dramatic *Millionaire* show music.

Have you ever watched the programme they made about the biggest game show fraud ever? It's amazing. This guy was totally obsessed with winning a million pounds, even though he didn't know much.

He blundered his way through the questions and it was really obvious he was cheating because one minute he'd say something like, 'I've never heard of Craig David,' and his mate would cough behind him. Then he'd say, 'Craig David is the correct answer.' And he'd win some more money.

I didn't know the answers to any of the questions, but I am only ten and I have never qualified to compete in *Who Wants to be a Millionaire?* – and never will – but this guy was at least thirty so he should have been brainy enough to answer the questions, especially if he had been eating enough spirulina.

The fraudster cheated his way through the rest of the questions until it came to THE million pound question, which was:

> *A number followed by one hundred zeroes is known by what name?*
>
> (A) *Googol*   (B) *Megatron*
> (C) *Gigabit*   (D) *Nanomole*

I happen to know that Megatron is a character in *Transformers*. But I didn't know which of the other three answers was correct.

The fraudster said, 'I don't actually know what a Googol is.' But in the end he chose it as his final answer and all this silvery stuff fell on him because he had won a million pounds.

'Let's give it a go,' Gordon said. 'Here is a question.'

> *In Greek mythology, who killed the Minotaur?*
>
> (A) *Daedalus*   (B) *Dionysus*
> (C) *Theseus*   (D) *Perseus*

'Do you know the answer?' asked Gordon.

'Of course not,' I said.

'Don't say that!' Freddo said. 'That's what gave the *Millionaire* fraudster away. He said he had no idea but still managed to get the question right in the end.'

He was right. I tried a different way.

'I think I might know the answer, but I'm not sure. Let me think.' I put my hand to my chin and tried to make out I was thinking really hard.

'It could be A: Dead-thingy.' Silence.

'Or maybe B: Dino-thingy.' Silence.

'I like the sound of C: This-thingy.'

Gordon put his hand over his mouth and coughed. Freddo coughed too.

'Sorry, I couldn't help myself,' he said and cleared his throat again.

Luckily I had heard when Gordon had coughed so I said, 'I think the answer is C. Final answer.'

'Congratulations! You just won a million pounds.' Freddo whooped. 'Chips all round.'

'He did not win a million pounds,' Gordon said. 'That was a hundred-pound question.'

'Still, a hundred pounds' worth of chips will do.'

'You are not getting chips ever again if you cough during the quiz,' I said.

'I didn't mean to cough. I had a tickle in my throat.' Freddo shrugged.

'I will do a more pointed cough, rather than a general cough,' Gordon said.

'What's a pointed cough?' I said.

Gordon gave a sharp bark into his hand.

We tried it out on a few questions. If Gordon knew the answer, he used his pointed cough. I ignored the spluttering coming from Freddo. Gordon and I got every question right. Suddenly, it felt this could really work. I was much cleverer than the Millionaire fraudster. I could win the Brainiac Championship and then maybe apply to *Who Wants to be a Millionaire* when this is all over and win a million pounds for real!

'Brilliant,' I said. 'We've got it nailed.'

'I think it's time to recreate studio conditions,' Gordon said. 'The cameras, the lights. A TV studio can be a very hot place, you know.'

Sometimes Gordon is a Genius. Sometimes he's a Geek and sometimes he's just a Goof (add it to the list). The 'recreating the studio conditions' idea

was one of his more stupid ideas.

He made me sit in the kitchen in front of the open oven door. He turned the heat up full blast and turned on every gas burner on the hob. I tried to tell him I didn't want to be a Barbecued Brainiac but he wouldn't listen. He shone Dad's desk lamp right in my face.

'I can't see a thing,' I said, screwing my eyes up against the blinding light.

'Good,' he said. 'Answer this question.'

What is the medical name for the part of the human body known as the 'windpipe'?

(A) *Trachea*   (B) *Spleen*

(C) *Humerus*   (D) *Fibula*

I was burning up and sweat dripped through my eyebrows, making my eyes sting.

Jessie bought me a can of antiperspirant deodorant for Christmas. It's called Aztec Dawn. I don't know how anyone knows what dawn smelt like in Aztec times but it's no wonder they died out as a race. One spray of that on Christmas morning

and I nearly asphyxiated my entire family.

So I hadn't used it since and now I was regretting it. I've never sweated so much in my life and a shot of Aztec Dawn was just what I needed.

'Dan, concentrate.' Gordon's voice sounded very distant. 'Look at me.'

I couldn't look at him because I couldn't see him. I couldn't really see anything except for brightness and darkness both at the same time. And it was very painful.

Gordon read the question and the multiple-choice answers again.

'Is it A?' My voice sounded slurred.

I think I heard a cough but I wasn't sure if it was pointed enough.

'Is it B?'

Cough.

I didn't know if I was imagining it.

'Is it C?'

Cough.

'Have you got something stuck in your windpipe? You're supposed to be telling me the right answer, not coughing at every option.'

'I am not,' Gordon said.

'Freddo is then.'

'Freddo has left the room,' Gordon said.

Cough. Cough.

'You're doing it again!'

'Mr Kendal, I assure you I am not coughing. I am not ill and I will only perform the pointed cough when you give me the correct option from the four choices.'

Cough.

Cough.

It's very difficult to concentrate when it feels like someone is sticking a pair of lightsabers in your eyeballs while you are being roasted alive by a powerful oven. And now my ears were full of imaginary coughing that sounded very real.

Timmy loomed out of the bright darkness. He leant on my knee and looked up at my face.

He coughed sharply, pointedly even, and put his hand over his mouth.

'It was you,' I said.

'Timmy got a cough.' He coughed again.

'He's imitating you, Gordon,' I said.

'Why?' Gordon said. He didn't have a younger brother. In fact, he didn't have any brothers or sisters at all.

Dad walked in. 'What's going on? It's boiling in here. Are you doing one of your weird science experiments again? Timmy, step away from the oven.'

Timmy toddled out of the room, coughing all the way.

'We're trying to recreate the conditions of a television studio,' Freddo said. 'It was Gordon's idea.'

'We're training your son to be a brainiac,' Gordon said.

'He doesn't need training. He's already very clever, aren't you, Dan? Well, at general knowledge, if not in lessons.' He put his arm around my sweaty shoulders and gave me a squeeze. 'I understand he even beat you, Gordon, so he must be clever.'

My cheeks flushed hot and it wasn't just the heat from the oven. Gordon's eyeballs pulsed as he tried to keep them in their sockets.

'Everyone in that quiz will be total geniuses,' Dad said. 'Or is that genii?'

'Geniuses,' Gordon said. 'Genii are the spirits that come out of bottles and grant you three wishes.'

I knew what I wished for right now: to go back in time and write my name on that test paper.

'It doesn't matter if you don't win,' Dad said. 'I'm just proud of you for representing your school.'

My toes curled in my size 49 trainers. He wouldn't be when I got caught cheating. We'd all be on the first plane to Albuquerque, to get away from the embarrassment.

Freddo coughed.

It sounded like a pointed cough but I wasn't trying to answer the questions, so I didn't know what he was on about.

Freddo coughed again and nodded towards my right leg.

I was so close to the oven, my jeans were smouldering. I was about to burst into flames.

'We're going outside. Fresh air is good for the brain,' I said and rushed out the back door. I ripped off my jeans and shoved them under the outdoor tap.

Freddo shut the back door so Dad wouldn't see me in my underpants and think we were

conducting some other dodgy science experiment.

'The coughing is no good,' I said. 'It's contagious. As soon as one person coughs everyone else starts up.'

I inspected my soggy jeans. There was a dark smudge on one leg but luckily it hadn't burnt right through. I'd just tell Dober-Mum I'd had an accident with a marker pen again.

'Hmm, yes. It's a well-recorded phenomenon.' Gordon consulted his laptop. 'One person coughs and others follow. It's like yawning. It's contagious, but without germs. I need to devise a method of communication that will not affect other people in the audience,' Gordon said. He closed his eyes and did his eyebrow-stroking routine again. 'Mobile phones,' he said.

'Do you really think they are going to let me take a mobile in to phone a friend at *The H-Factor*?'

'What if they don't know you've got one?' Gordon said.

16

A Real

Buzz

Gordon's idea was pretty neat.

Four mobile phones, set to vibrate, would be strapped to my body.

*The question
master asks
the question.*

*Gordon texts
the correct phone.*

*The phone buzzes
with the text.*

I have the right answer.

But nothing is ever simple in my life.

We needed five mobiles. One for each answer and one to text the answers from.

Phone 1 – Gordon's iPhone. Top of the range. The latest model. He was going to use this phone to text the answers.

Phone 2 – the chemical symbol iPhone Gordon had lent me. Gordon was prepared to let me strap it to my back as long as I disinfected it afterwards.

Phone 3 – Freddo has the latest phone that looks like an iPhone but isn't.

I have to make do with two tin cans and a piece of string to communicate.

Well, not exactly but my phone is so old it can't take pictures or surf the web. It does receive texts though so it was going to have to do.

Phone 4 – my ancient, out-of-date brick.

However even with my antique, we were one phone short.

'If you don't receive a buzz in the backside, you'll know the answer is D,' Freddo said.

'That's no good,' I said. 'I might think Gordon doesn't know the answer.'

'Will you, Mr Kendal?' Gordon peered at me

over his glasses like a stuck-up professor.

'Sorry, mate, but you don't know EVERYTHING.'

'I know my name, which is more than you do,' Gordon said. He really hates being called 'mate'. 'Do you want my help or not?'

'Of course I do. All I'm saying is I'd feel happier if I had a phone for every option.'

'We could use your sister's phone,' Freddo said.

'Are you mad? Jessie's phone is permanently super-glued to her ear.'

'Does she take it in the shower?' Gordon said. He opened the bedroom door and we could all hear the sound of the shower along with One Dimension playing at full blast from the bathroom.

'I reckon we've got ten minutes, tops,' I said. 'I'll get her phone. You sort out how to stick the others to my body.'

Jessie's room is a total shrine to One Dimension. I think the room is painted pastel pink, but you'd never know. The walls are covered completely with posters. It was a bit creepy having five pairs of eyes watching me from every bit of the room. Particularly when I was on such an illegal mission.

'Don't worry, guys,' I said to the band when I picked up Jessie's phone from the bed. 'I'm only borrowing it. Back in a minute.'

What was happening to me? I was now talking to pictures of One Dimension. Jessie was having a very bad influence on me.

We laid the four phones out on the carpet and decided which one was A, B, C and D.

Gordon wouldn't actually touch me so he got Freddo to strap the phones to my back.

Jessie's fake diamond-encrusted blingy cover itched like a zillion crazy mosquito bites on my skin, but I didn't have time to rip the case off her phone right now. The minutes were ticking away.

My T-shirt covered the phones pretty well. I looked like I had a spinal deformity but I reckon I could get away with it as the competition organisers were adults and adults don't normally ask awkward questions of kids with obvious disabilities. If anyone did ask, I'd tell them I'd strapped my teddy to my back for good luck.

Freddo was question master this time as Gordon was texting the answers.

Which of these islands is in the Mediterranean Sea?

Before he had given me the answers the Jessie's phone buzzed giving me a nasty scrape.

'D,' I said.

'Wrong,' Freddo said.

'Gordon, don't text me the answer until they give me the options otherwise they'll know I'm cheating.'

'I didn't,' he said.

Jessie's phone buzzed again. I tried to swat the itchy thing away.

Then the phone on my left shoulder buzzed.

'Is it A?' I said.

'No. The answer is B, Crete,' Freddo said.

'Who is texting me then?'

'Turn round,' Freddo said and he pulled up the back of my T-shirt to read the text messages. 'Dazzer wants to meet Jessie on the corner at six o'clock, and PVZ say I've qualified for a free upgrade. Awesome.' Freddo ripped his phone off my back, taking a large patch of skin with it.

'That hurt! This is hopeless. We need four

brand-new phones with four brand-new numbers so I don't keep getting messages from *Plants Vs Zombies* or Jessie's boyfriend.'

Jessie's phone vibrated again, only this time it wasn't a text, it was a call with a very loud One Dimension ringtone as well as the vibration. Didn't know what song – they all sound the same to me.

'Anyone hear my phone?' Jessie wailed from the landing. 'I've lost it.'

Rat's bum! I ripped the phone and its itchy cover off my back. I had to give it back. Jessie was going to go mental when she realised I'd borrowed it. But she'd go even more mental if she found it ringing in my room and I didn't give it to her. I decided the best option was to return it to her as quickly as possible.

'Take cover!' I shouted. 'She's about to go nuclear!' I threw the bling phone out onto the landing like a live grenade.

'I'm going to kill you, Daniel Kendal!' Jessie screamed. I just had a glimpse of Jessie dressed in a towel, her hair dripping everywhere, flying towards me, before I slammed my bedroom door in her angry face.

'Barricade! Barricade!' I shouted.

Freddo knew the drill. We'd been here many times before. He threw himself against the door while I dragged the chest of drawers across to stop her from pushing it open. We both sat on the top.

'Daniel!' Jessie wailed. But her One Dimension ringtone rang out again and she gave up immediately. I guess speaking to her boyfriend was more urgent than killing her brother.

It was good to know I was going to live another day.

'We need another phone,' I said. 'Any chance, Freddo?'

Freddo was about to answer when Gordon stopped him.

'I may have made a miscalculation.' Gordon's eyeballs started throbbing in their sockets. 'This method will only work if the questions are multiple choice.'

'But the questions *are* multiple choice, aren't they?' I said. Panic gripped my stomach.

Gordon stared endlessly at a piece of Blu-Tack on the wall above my bed. Then he took out his laptop and tapped away at a zillion miles an hour.

Eventually he looked up and whispered, 'No. The questions are not all multiple choice.'

There was a thick, black empty silence in the room. Bigger than the great cavernous nothingness in my brain. We had to come up with a foolproof plan if I was going to stand any chance of getting a single question right, let alone win.

'What happened to the *Millionaire* fraudster, anyway?' I asked.

'Jail,' Freddo said. 'Eighteen months.'

17

Ouch!

'I don't want to go to jail,' I said. 'I wouldn't fit in.'

1. I don't have a tattoo.
*2. I hate the colour grey. (Everything is grey
in jail. Even the food.)*
3. I don't know enough swear words.

'I need to cheat without anyone finding out.'

'No point looking at me,' Freddo said. 'I know nothing. Remember?'

'Any ideas, Gordon?' I said.

Gordon closed his eyes and rested his hands on his keyboard. His skinny chest rose as he took a

deep breath in and sank beneath his blazer as he blew the air out of his pursed lips. He did it again. Each breath seemed to take for ever.

Freddo folded his arms across his chest. I knew what he was thinking.

Gordon was acting weirder than normal. Although this time it didn't involve his eyebrows.

Gordon breathed in again. As he exhaled, he gently brushed his fingers across the keyboard of his laptop. He wasn't typing. It was more like . . . dusting. Only there was no dust on his ultra-clean laptop. His fingers changed to moving in a circular motion but he didn't open his eyes.

'Didn't know you did massage,' Freddo said.

Gordon opened one eyelid and bulged his eyeball in Freddo's direction.

'Reiki,' Gordon said and I could see his other eyelid fluttering as if he was about to open it.

'What's that?' Freddo said.

'I think Gordon needs quiet,' I said, willing Freddo to shut up.

Gordon put his eyeball away and returned to stroking the keyboard.

'I need food. Got any crisps?' Freddo said.

I sensed Gordon tense. The only way I could get Freddo to shut up was to stuff food in his mouth.

Remember Dober-Mum's rules? No food upstairs. Luckily I have a secret supply of snacks at the back of my wardrobe. But all I had left were brainiac rice cakes. I opened the packet behind my back so Freddo couldn't see what I was about to feed him.

'Open wide!' I said.

Freddo took up position.

I threw one of the ricey polystyrene discs over Gordon's head into Freddo's open mouth.

Freddo's jaws snapped shut but a millisecond later they were open again and a damp rice cake flew out at a zillion miles an hour.

A rare instinct kicked in at that moment and I launched myself across the room to bat the saliva-covered snack away from Gordon.

It worked.

Sort of.

Gordon didn't get contaminated by Freddo's rejected rice cake but my foot accidently got caught in the cable of his precious laptop and ripped it off his lap. The lid snapped shut and the machine spun across the carpet like a low-flying Frisbee. Gordon

leapt to his feet and snatched the spinning laptop off the floor.

'Hands off!' he shrieked.

'Sorry!' I held my hands up.

Gordon cradled the laptop to his chest like a well-loved teddy. I suspect Gordon doesn't have a teddy because of the germs. He probably never did. The laptop was his most treasured possession.

'I was trying to protect you from this.' I opened my hand and showed him the crumpled slimy rice cake in the palm of my hand.

Gordon turned a weird green colour and backed into a corner.

'What is it?' he said.

'Yeah, what were you trying to poison me with?' Freddo said and he wiped his tongue on the sleeve of his T-shirt. 'It tasted disgustingly healthy to me.'

'Leftovers from the brainiac diet,' I muttered. 'Is your laptop okay?'

Gordon lifted the lid a little and looked inside. He nodded.

'What were you doing anyway?' Freddo said.

'Reiki. A form of Japanese spiritual healing. I've been experimenting with using it as a divination

method to obtain information from the internet.'

'What's wrong with Google?' Freddo said.

'Google is a computer program. It has filters and algorithms created by humans that might block important information from me.'

Freddo smirked. We'd had a session at school on cyber-security and all the stuff adults didn't think we should know about on the internet.

'Did the reiki thing work?' I asked.

'I doubt it. You interrupted the flow of ki,' Gordon said.

I didn't know what he was talking about but I felt guilty anyway.

Gordon looked at the screen. Suddenly his face lit up.

'I think your intervention may have been fortuitous after all. When you kicked the laptop, I must have instinctively pressed a button, or you knocked the trackpad or something.' He tapped feverishly away. 'Yes! Yes! Yes!' he said in his soppy 'computer-I-love-you' voice. 'That's it!' A broad grin spread over his face.

Gordon had to explain his idea seven times before Freddo and I understood it. He even drew us a diagram.

*The question
master asks
the question.*

*Gordon in the audience
answers in a pinhead
microphone attached
to his sleeve*

*Answer is transmitted
to a speaker embedded
in the arm of
Dan's glasses*

Dan speaks the answer.

'But I'll be wearing a speaker. What if other people hear your voice too as it whispers in my ear?'

'That's the clever thing.' Gordon's cheeks flushed pink. 'The device on you doesn't make a sound. It uses an awesome technology called bone conduction. The glasses transmit tiny vibrations that your brain is able to hear. You will be able to hear it, but no one else will.'

'Vibrating glasses?' Freddo said.

You would have thought Freddo would have total faith in Gordon by now. But you'd be wrong. Luckily I knew Gordon better than Freddo.

'I have everything I need at home to make the glasses,' Gordon said as he scribbled something on a piece of paper. 'You source the microphone.' He handed the paper to Freddo.

'Thank you, Gordon. You are a genius,' I said.

18

The H-Factor

The National Brainiac Championship was being held at Dad's university – the one where he teaches brainy people to be even more brainy. Normally, you have to have a brain the size of Jupiter just to get a visitor's pass. My brain had shrivelled to the size of a gobstopper but the security guard didn't seem to notice. He let me, Mum, Dad and Jessie through the gates without getting his tape measure out.

'Good morning, Mr Daniels.' Mr Biggend's voice boomed across the reception area. 'What a triumph! Kenny in the finals.' He slapped me on the back and smiled in that totally fake way he saved for parents.

Dad frowned.

Mum frowned.

Jessie laughed.

I think my family were very confused that Mr Biggend didn't know my name. He'd been my head teacher for six years and Kendal is not a difficult name to remember. It's easy to spell and easy to say. I'd also told them that Mr Biggend had won the very first National Brainiac Championship when he was at school. I could tell they thought a supposed brainiac like him should remember my name. Especially as it was his job.

'Here is the rest of Kenny's year, ready to cheer him on.' Mr Biggend waved at a group of Year 6s who were being supervised by Mr Pitdown. Rooners made a rude sign. He hadn't forgiven me for refusing to do his homework. He'd hate me even more if he found out I was planning to cheat in the quiz.

'The contestants and their families are to wait in the small cafeteria,' announced a short woman with a tight skirt and high heels, ushering us with her clipboard. 'Everyone else is to go through to the theatre. Please remember to turn off your mobile phones.'

Freddo gave me the thumbs-up and Gordon

pointed to the cufflink microphone he had ready.

I took Gordon's cheating glasses out of my pocket to show I was ready.

'You better sit with me, Gordon,' Mr Pitdown said. 'Let's see if we can answer the questions before Daniel.'

I froze. Gordon sitting next to Mr Pitdown was not part of the plan.

'I promised Gordon I'd sit next to him,' Freddo said and let out a pointed cheese-and-onion burp in Mr Pitdown's face. 'Pardon me,' he said for the first time ever.

Mr Pitdown wrinkled his nose and nodded before turning away.

Nice one, Freddo! My two best friends disappeared into the auditorium together.

Dad led the way to the waiting area for the contestants.

Did you know brainiacs come in all shapes and sizes? I might have been taller than most other kids but, believe me, I looked normal compared to every other contestant in that competition.

What do you call a crowd of brainiacs? Something like weird, freaky or odd.

Reasons why I didn't belong here

1. I was the only competitor without a tie. I was wearing jeans and a T-shirt.

2. My head was miles smaller than everyone else's. I bet Gordon's brain-growth chart would have been blown out of the water if he had plugged their measurements into his spreadsheet.

3. They were ALL wearing the exact same style glasses as Gordon's. I mean his real ones.

4. I was wearing his cheating specs made from a pair of his granddad's old glasses. The frames were far too big and kept slipping down my nose. Gordon's granddad obviously had a big head too. It must run in the family.

I sat as far away from the other kids as I possibly could in case even they asked me something I couldn't answer. I was trying to avoid humiliation at all costs.

'What are those?' Jessie pointed at my face, as we sat waiting to go into the auditorium.

'Do you want me to win or not?' I said.

'Are they X-ray specs, then? So you can see the answers written on the other side of the question card? That is your only chance of winning.' Jessie took a photo of me with her phone. No doubt it was on Facebook within seconds even though all phones were supposed to be switched off.

'Leave him alone, Jessie,' Mum said. 'Did Gordon give you those for good luck, Dan?'

'Something like that,' I said.

'They make you look very distinguished,' Mum said.

'They make you look like a dork,' Jessie said. Another word for the NOT-brainiac list.

I caught a glimpse of myself in a mirror as I walked into the theatre. I didn't look like a distinguished dork. I looked like a lying cheat. And I felt pretty sick about it.

The university theatre had been converted into a TV studio for the day. There were lights and cameras everywhere, but luckily they were pointing at the stage and not the audience, so Gordon didn't need to get paranoid about them draining the power from his precious brain cells. The stage was built out into the audience and each contestant had to stand behind a tall, thin podium, a bit like the thing that holds the Bible in a church. We were arranged in a horseshoe-shape around the question master's tall table. I was between Spooky Brain and Barbie Brain.

My guts were going flipping mental. Or was that flipping mentally? What if Mr Pitdown had forced Gordon to sit next to him after all? I couldn't see into the audience because of the lights. Gordon needed to be free to speak into his cufflink microphone. I couldn't do this on my own.

The question master was Max Novel, the brainiest brainiac in the country. He had even less hair than Dad so I could see the ridges on his bald head where his massive brain was trying to bust out of his skull. I bet he had a permanent headache.

A woman with big hair and a big nose sat next to him. She didn't speak. Max Novel introduced her

as the referee but I couldn't see a whistle hanging around her neck.

Someone with a clipboard explained about the lights and the cameras. They also made the audience practise clapping. I practised trying not to be sick.

'Lights. Camera. Action.' And the recording began.

Max Novel said hello in that fake gameshow-host way and told the audience all about the show. Then he turned towards me and the other competitors and explained the rules of the competition.

'There will be random questions across all branches of general knowledge. Press your buzzer to answer. Make sure you answer correctly or not at all. As soon as you get a question wrong you will be eliminated. If you fail to answer a question at least every five questions, you will be eliminated. The last contestant standing will be the winner.'

The audience clapped. My guts leapt up and wrapped themselves round my throat. He meant that I couldn't sit there saying nothing. I had to keep answering questions to stay in the quiz.

Bright lights zoomed to and fro in front of my glasses. Sweat trickled down my forehead, making the cheating glasses slip even lower. I grabbed the frame and jammed it against my head.

'You all right, Dan?' Freddo's voice filled my brain.

'I am in charge of the microphone.' Gordon's voice now.

It was as if my head was my bedroom and the three of us were hanging out, chatting as normal. Only I wasn't at home. I was on the stage with a massive TV camera focusing on my face and my two best friends were out there in the darkness of the audience.

'Can't you see he's panicking?' Freddo said.

'Give the microphone to me,' Gordon said. My head filled with a deafening fumble. They must have been fighting over the microphone. Everything went quiet until Gordon's voice said, 'It is time to relax. Breathe in. Breathe out.'

It was amazing. My shoulders relaxed and suddenly I was able to breathe and see straight. The glasses didn't just tell me what to do, they actually made me do it. It was as if Gordon's thoughts became my thoughts. I was relaxing because he wanted me to. So as long as he knew the answers to the questions, I was going to be all right.

'Nice one,' Freddo whooped and my glasses vibrated so violently it felt like a freight train had run over my head.

'Please refrain from touching my blazer,' Gordon said. Only he wasn't talking to me. Obviously.

'Okay, contestants, it's time to begin,' Max Novel said. 'Question One . . .'

19

Question Me

to Destruction

'Grurrghhh!'

An ogre burped in the cave of my empty brain drowning out the question. Only it wasn't an ogre. It was Freddo ruining everything.

Zany Brain buzzed in and said, 'Palaeontology'.

The question must have been something about dinosaurs. I probably would have been able to answer it, if only Freddo had kept his burping mouth shut.

'Correct!' Max Novel said. 'Why are—'

'You are so disgusting!' Gordon hissed in my ear.

Jumpy Brain buzzed.

'Pointillism.'

I wasn't sure if it was a word or a sneeze.

The glasses slipped down my sweaty nose and at last I got to hear a question.

'Which birds belong to the order Strigiformes?'

I hadn't a clue. I waited for Gordon's voice to appear in my ear but he didn't say anything. Maybe he didn't know the answer.

'Owls,' Snaky Brain answered.

'Correct.'

This was impossible. I either didn't get to hear the questions or I didn't know the answers because Gordon was too busy fighting with Freddo to speak to me. I pushed the glasses back up my face.

'I think you should see a doctor.' Gordon's voice again. 'Bad breath can be an indication of poor digestive health.'

'Don't you like it?' Freddo had that hint of glee in his voice that meant he was enjoying winding Gordon up. He was never going to shut up now. 'Huuuuuuuuuuuuuuh!' Freddo breathed out very loudly.

'Stay back! I have highly developed olfactory perception,' Gordon's voice squeaked in my ear. I didn't know what he was on about but it was obvious both my best friends had forgotten about

me and the competition.

'Question Five,' Max Novel said. 'Anyone who hasn't answered a question yet needs to answer this question or you will be out of the competition. That's you Dimitri, Florence and Daniel.' He meant Fishy, Barbie and me.

'Grurrghhh!' Freddo burped again. I didn't need cheating glasses to hear it. The sound echoed all around the auditorium. But because of the cheating glasses the sound was so loud it nearly blew my head off.

I snatched the glasses off my face just in time to hear the crucial question.

'What is the middle name of Captain James T Kirk of the *Starship Enterprise*?'

I slammed my buzzer.

'Tiberius,' I said. And I knew I was . . .

'Correct!'

The crowd clapped and I felt the glasses vibrate on the podium.

'I'm sorry, Florence and Dimitri, you have to leave the competition.'

Fishy Brain walked off the stage. Big tears plopped out of his eyes into his gaping mouth as he struggled

for air. He hadn't answered a single question.

Barbie Brain flicked her ponytail and swung her hips like a catwalk model as she walked away. She gave the audience a little wave and everyone cheered. Someone wolf-whistled and Barbie curtsied before leaving her fans for good.

I'd got an answer right!

Me!

All on my own!

The glasses vibrated like crazy. I bet Gordon and Freddo were yelling at me to put them back on. But I didn't want to. I was no longer taking part in *The H-Factor*. I was in the National Brainiac Championship and even if I didn't know another question I wouldn't be the first person to leave the competition.

I had never wanted to cheat. I might not have inherited the brainy gene from my parents but I was a true Kendal when it came to honesty.

Max Novel asked the next question. I didn't know what he was talking about but I leant down and placed my cheating glasses by my feet. I didn't need them any more. I could answer the questions on my own.

20

The Final

Showdown

The questions kept flying. Zany Brain answered most of them, closely followed by Snaky and Spooky. I stood quietly knowing that I would be out of the competition if I didn't answer another question soon.

'Name the five original members of One Dimension.'

My hand shot out and smacked the buzzer as hard as Jessie would smack me if I got this question wrong.

'Zak Mandrake, Hazzer Stanton, Luigi Topper, Neil Horror, Lee Potter.'

'Correct!'

'That's my brother!' Jessie screamed from the audience. 'We love One Dimension!'

A jeer came from another part of the audience and my cheating glasses jiggled against my shoe. Freddo was never going to let me forget that.

I shrank down behind my podium and willed myself to disappear. But at least Jessie had helped me get a question right.

Jumpy and Crusty were eliminated.

'Which monument stands in London's Trafalgar Square?'

I knew it! I'd been there on holiday last year! But when I went to answer, Snaky Brain buzzed in first.

'Nelson's Column.' She looked over and stuck her tongue out at me. It wasn't forked. She was a fake, not a snake.

Right! I was going to show her. I could beat a fake snake any day of the week. All I had to do was get my hand on that buzzer first.

'A number followed by one hundred zeroes is known by what name?' Max Novel asked.

BUZZZZZZZZZZZ.

'A googol,' I said.

'Correct.'

Thank you, the *Millionaire* fraudster. If you hadn't cheated, that question would never have appeared on *Who Wants to be a Millionaire?* and I would never have known the answer. I hadn't won a million pounds, but I was still in the quiz.

This was fun. I didn't need to cheat. I actually knew some of the answers and I didn't care whether I won or lost.

My family would be proud of me. I didn't buckle under pressure.

My friends would be thrilled. I was a TV superstar.

Mr Pitdown would go mental that I had proved him wrong.

Mr Biggend might reinstate Maths Day, though. On the other hand he might not. It didn't matter.

And most important of all, I was showing the whole

world I wasn't a stupid bozo numbskull.

Spooky Brain got an answer wrong, so then it was just Snaky Brain, Zany Brain and me – Not Much Brain. But it seemed I had just enough to be in this competition.

'What is the opening line of the Queen song "Bohemian Rhapsody"?'

The words Dad had sung came out of my mouth so instinctively, I wasn't sure if I spoke them or sang them. No one laughed so I think I got away with it. Before I could blink, Max Novel fired off the next question.

'What is the chemical symbol for potassium?'

All three of us slammed our hands on the buzzer but it was Zany who got there first.

'K,' she said.

I knew it was K! That was an easy one.

'What is reiki?' asked Max.

What was going on? These were my questions. All of them. Gordon and Freddo's coaching had paid off. I was now brainy enough to answer these questions. I knew what reiki was but I didn't get a chance to buzz in with my answer, 'A method of surfing the internet.'

That evil Snaky got in first.

'A type of moth,' she said.

'Incorrect,' Max Novel said. 'The answer is a type of Japanese spiritual healing. You are eliminated.'

Of course! Gordon had told me that. He was only experimenting with reiki as a type of internet surfing

'Noooooooooooooo!' Snaky Brain wailed. 'I thought you said *ringlet*.' Her eyeballs turned lime green and her pupils changed into narrow slits. I'd been wrong about the fake snake thing.

'Ask me another question. Ask me anything. If I get it wrong, I'll leave. Give me another chance.'

The producers asked the cameras

to stop recording. A hum of annoyance rippled through the audience. I looked across at Zany Brain and rolled my eyes. She ran her finger over each eyebrow in turn, checked her hair wasn't sticking out over her ears and wrinkled her nose before looking away. The exact same routine Gordon had been hooked on for the last two weeks. She was a female version of Gordon, only with hair gel and black eyeliner. How weird! Maybe she was his twin sister and they had been separated at birth.

Max Novel and the referee-without-a-whistle came over to speak to Snaky.

'I'm afraid your time at the National Brainiac Championship is over,' Max Novel said.

Snaky wrapped her arms around her body and poked out her tongue. I think it *was* forked this time.

'According to regulation 3.2.1 in the competition rules,' the referee said in a low, calm voice, 'you are eliminated because you answered a question incorrectly. You must therefore leave the competition.'

'Make me!' Snaky hissed. She plucked some pins out of her hair and the coils quickly unravelled.

I shut my eyes in case she was a gorgon trying to

turn us all to stone. But when no one screamed in terror, I opened them again.

Snaky Brain wasn't a gorgon. She was just a brainiac desperate to stay in the quiz. She wrapped her long ropey hair to her podium and tied the ends in a double knot.

'*Why are we waiting?*' a familiar voice chanted from the audience. My cheating specs vibrated against my foot. It was Freddo.

'*We are suffocating,*' Gordon sang out.

He probably *was* suffocating – from Freddo's stinking burps.

The audience started a long, slow clap. I don't think Snaky realised everyone was asking her to leave.

It took four security guards to lift the screaming girl and her podium out of the auditorium. The slow clap accelerated into a round of applause as she disappeared through the theatre doors and her screams were smothered by industrial sound-proofing.

That left Zany Brain. And me. The final two.

21

The

Grand Final

'Congratulations, Arabella and Daniel,' Max Novel said once the cameras were rolling again.

Zany Brain was called Arabella! She didn't look like an Arabella. She looked like a Sid.

'In the final round, the rules are slightly different,' Max Novel continued. 'If one of you answers a question incorrectly you will NOT be eliminated immediately. I will ask the same question to the remaining contestant. If that contestant answers incorrectly then neither will be eliminated and I will ask another question. If, however, the second contestant answers the question correctly, they will be the winner.'

So, if I buzzed in and got the question wrong, I might not be out if Zany didn't know the answer either. But Zany was much brainier than me. She probably knew everything.

'Are you ready?' Max Novel said.

'Please proceed,' Zany said.

Wow. She even spoke like Gordon.

I just nodded. My mouth was too dry to say anything.

'What is Hanukkah?'

I hadn't a clue.

Zany Brain buzzed in and said, 'A middle eastern sweet made from sesame.'

That was it. The end of the quiz. I'd lost. But it didn't matter. I'd done better than anyone could have hoped. Only Mr Biggend would be disappointed and to be honest I didn't care about him as he didn't even know my name.

'Incorrect!' Max Novel said.

Whoa! A rush of something powerful shot through my body and it wasn't trapped wind. More like a shot of awesomeness!

The audience murmured. Arabella Zany Brain had been the strongest contestant in the competition.

She'd known everything up until now.

The only problem was, I didn't know the answer either.

'Daniel, you may answer the question. What is Hanukkah?'

'Pass,' I said in a husky voice that sounded like someone else.

'Incorrect. Hanukkah is a festival in the Jewish religion,' Max Novel said.

I wasn't a brainiac, that was for sure, but right now Zany wasn't either.

She was a bozo numbskull like me.

None of the contestants knew everything. We all knew stuff. They knew some stuff. I knew other stuff. No one knew it all. Not even Gordon.

Gordon wouldn't recognise the members of One Dimension if they walked in the room now, for instance. I would. Even Timmy would know who they are. Jessie would wet her pants.

No one knows everything. There is no such thing as a total brainiac.

'Next question. Which city in New Mexico, USA, has two "q"s in its name?'

Ha! I slammed the buzzer but Zany got there first.

'Algonquin,' she said out loud but immediately scewed up her face with agony. 'One q,' she muttered.

No way! She had got it wrong and I knew the answer!

'That is incorrect. Daniel, can you answer the question?' Max

Novel looked at me.

I knew the answer but my brain suddenly froze. I could see the place name on the map. I could see Big Willie Bragman's red face. I could hear Jessie telling me she didn't want to move to . . .

'Al-al-alber-quickly,' I stuttered.

That didn't sound right. The room went all wobbly around me. I grabbed hold of the podium in front of me in case I fainted.

Max Novel whispered to the referee sitting next to him. She shook her head. Max Novel nodded.

'I'm sorry, Daniel, but that is incorrect. The correct answer is Albuquerque. Your pronunciation wasn't close enough.'

'Next question. Give me a close approximation of pi—'

Zany buzzed in.

'3.147.' She looked triumphant as she recited the number Gordon had told me before.

Of course she was right. All brainiacs knew the value of pi to a zillion decimal places. It was only NOT-brainiacs like me who didn't know.

There was a deep hush in the auditorium as the whole audience held their breath, expecting Max

Novel to declare Zany Brain as the winner.

But for some reason Max Novel consulted the adjudicator again. She put her fingers to her forehead and closed her eyes while she muttered under her breath. Max Novel nodded.

'I'm sorry, Arabella, that is not correct,' Max Novel said.

'Yes, it is!' Arabella said.

'You interrupted before I had completed the question and therefore answered incorrectly.'

Arabella snorted. I wasn't looking but I could smell smoke.

Max Novel turned to me. The lights in the auditorium dimmed even lower and a spotlight shone right in my face. The light was blinding and hot. I couldn't see anything but everyone could see me. But I was used to it. These were exactly the conditions we had rehearsed in front of the oven.

'Daniel, if you answer this question correctly you will be the National Brainiac Champion.'

It was a very big IF.

Arabella Zany Brain had got it wrong. So what was the full question? I still didn't understand what

this pi thing was. I was never going to know the answer. I wasn't going to win. I knew that. But I couldn't lose either. If I answered the question wrong, me and Zany over there would have another question to answer. There was no way my luck would hold out for ever. She was going to end up winning this competition but I didn't care.

Max Novel cleared his throat and asked the full question.

'Give me a close approximation of the value of pi – as a fraction.'

My guts clenched in a furious twist. I hated fractions! Gordon had talked about pi as a decimal. That string of numbers Zany had spewed out. But she was wrong. There must have been another value but I'd been too busy joking with Freddo to listen properly. Gordon had some crazy phrase that helped him to remember the number. It had alcohol in but he was far too young to drink and he probably never would drink alcohol as it would kill off too many of his precious brain cells. And anyway, that was a decimal, not a fraction. A fraction is one number over another.

'I need an answer,' Max Novel said. 'You can

pass if you want to.'

Freddo drew something, didn't he? Something to do with bingo.

I closed my eyes and searched through my shrivelled brain just like I'd seen Gordon do a hundred times.

I could see Freddo drawing a picture of a bird. No – a duck! Two ducks!

My eyes snapped open. I knew the answer. Two little ducks over the lucky number.

'Twenty-two over seven!' I said the words, but Gordon and Freddo had put them there. Not through the cheating glasses, but by being there when I needed them.

They didn't like each other much. Put them on their own together with an important mission to complete, they'd fight. But when the three of us were together, we were a team. A brilliant team.

'Twenty-two over seven is . . .' Max Novel did that annoying thing they did on all TV quizzes. The dramatic pause. But I wasn't worried. I knew my answer was correct thanks to my two best friends.

'Correct,' Max Novel said. 'Daniel Kendal, you are this year's National Brainiac Champion!'

22

Brainiacs

R Us

The audience went mental. I couldn't see them because every spotlight in the room was shining in my eyes but I could hear everyone clapping and whistling. In amongst it all I heard Freddo shout, 'AWESOME!' and Gordon squeaked, 'BRAVO!'

They were all cheering for me. Daniel Kendal.

The Brainiac.

How weird is that?

Arabella Zany Brain stood up next to me. Her punky hair had fallen flat and her black make-up streaked down her cheeks. It had either melted under the lights or she'd been crying. She looked like a damp zebra.

'Bad luck,' I said. 'You were great.' I held out my hand to shake hers.

She pulled on some leather fingerless gloves before she took my hand and even then she didn't let the tips of her fingers touch my skin.

'Not as great as you,' she said in a robotic voice. She nodded once and walked away. I think she went to fix her make-up.

The TV crew sprang into action. They rearranged the cameras and lights and some of the furniture. I was pushed onto a little platform at the front of the stage. A woman with frizzy hair and glittery eyeshadow dapped my face with a tissue then covered it with skin-coloured powder. Her friend dragged a comb through my hair.

Max Novel said something but I couldn't hear so I nodded and grinned like an idiot. He shoved a large wooden shield into my hands. And the audience cheered all over again.

I didn't know what to do. I'd never been a Brainiac before.

But it didn't matter because all of a sudden the show was over. The TV lights went off, the normal lights came on and suddenly everyone I cared about

was on the stage with me (except Timmy who was at nursery).

Dad hugged me.

Mum hugged me.

Jessie called me Dan the Man.

Freddo hugged me. I'm going to give him my can of Aztec Dawn. He needs it.

Gordon hugged me very briefly, without actually touching me.

'I'll tell them to put your name on the shield, Gordon,' I said. 'I couldn't have done it without you.'

'That is not required, Daniel,' he said. 'You won. You are the champion.'

'Thanks, mate. I mean, Gordon. I mean, Mr Franks. I might be this year's champion but you are the all-time genius.'

I put up my hand for a high five. Gordon raised his hand too. He took a very deep breath, closed his eyes and quickly swiped his palm across mine.

'Did you get any cash with that shield?' Freddo said. 'You still owe me ten quid and I'm starving.'

'Sorry, Freddo,' I said. 'I only get this and you can't eat it.' I held up the shield.

'Smile!' Jessie said and she took a picture of Team Brainiac with her phone.

I hope she puts it on Facebook.

Mr Biggend and Mr Pitdown joined us on the stage. Mr Biggend's smile took up his whole face. Mr Pitdown's lips were super-glued together so he couldn't smile.

'Congratulations, Mr and Mrs Daniels,' Mr Biggend said. He still didn't know our name. 'What an achievement! The National Brainiac shield is going to be returned to where it belongs: my school.' He grabbed the shield out of my hands. He stared lovingly at it, admiring his reflection in the silver bits studded over the surface.

'That's Daniel's!' Jessie snatched the shield out of Mr Biggend's hands. 'It's going on our Shrine of Achievement at home where it truly belongs.'

'Congratulations, Daniel.' Mr Pitdown prised his lips open enough to speak. 'A truly re-mark-able achievement.' He raised his Spocky eyebrow at me.

'Isn't he brilliant?' Mum hugged me again.

'Isn't he?' Mr Pitdown said.

Somehow I knew that Mr Pitdown did not think I was brilliant. He thought I was a cheat and he was accusing me of cheating right in front of Mum!

'Good thing I taught you the middle name of Captain James T Kirk,' he said. 'Otherwise you

would have been the first to be eliminated.'

Freddo stepped forward and put his arm around me.

'Even I know that,' he said. 'You don't have to have plastic ears to know about *Star Trek*.'

Mr Pitdown blushed. Definitely no Vulcan blood in him.

'I think we better go home,' Mum said. 'Dad and I have got a shelf to put up.'

23

When Is a Brainiac
Not a Brainiac?

I woke up the next morning feeling like a true member of the Kendal family for the first time ever. I was going to tell Freddo that the NOT-brainiac competition was over. I quite liked being clever for a change. Maybe, when I'm an adult, I could be a university lecturer like Dad. Only I might have to make *Star Trek* or *The Beano* my specialist subject.

Dad stood at the cooker flipping pancakes. Mum was juicing oranges. These were the ingredients to a Kendal celebration breakfast.

'Would you like spirulina with your orange juice?' Mum winked at me.

'No, thank you. I think I've got enough brain cells.'

'You certainly have.' Mum smiled as she shoved the next orange into the juicer. 'You proved that yesterday in front of the world.'

'Dad?' Jessie said. 'You said Dan could have whatever he wanted if he won. What does he get?'

'What do you want, Dan?' Dad muttered. He looked across at Mum who raised her Dober-Mum eyebrows at him.

Jessie kicked me under the table.

'I could really do with a laptop,' I said.

Jessie kicked me harder.

'But I guess I'll have to wait until we move to America. In case it's different voltage over there or something.'

'About America,' Dad said. 'How would you all feel if we stayed here?'

Mum burst into tears.

'Liz? Honey?' Dad said and he pulled Mum in for a hug. 'When we were at the university yesterday, I spoke to the head of department and he has offered me a promotion here. So I was thinking . . . we could stay. But if you really want to emigrate, I could turn them down.'

'I don't want to emigrate!' Mum wailed. 'I want to stay here!'

'I thought you wanted to go to America?' Dad said.

'For a holiday!' Mum said. 'Not for ever!'

'You never said!' Dad hugged her tight then kissed her full on the lips. Yuk!

Luckily I heard some post drop through the letter box at that moment so I used it as an excuse to leave the table.

There was only one letter. It was addressed to me.

'That's weird,' I said. 'It's got a USA stamp on it.'

Dear Daniel Kendal,

Congratulations on being this year's Brainiac Champion for your nation.

I am delighted to invite you and your family here to the USA on an all-expenses paid trip

YES! How amazing would that be!
I read on.

> to the World Brainiac
> Championships next year,
> which will be held in
> Albuquerque, New Mexico.

NO!
I'm not a brainiac!
HELP!

Coming soon . . .

Help! I'm a Detective!

Being the middle one in the family totally
sucks. Daniel gets the blame for everything.
A series of burglaries in the street gives him
the perfect opportunity to prove himself.
Once again he asks Freddo and
Gordon the Geek for help, but are
the three friends really cut out
to be crimebusters?

Don't miss more **Help!** mayhem!

Help! I'm an Alien

Daniel Kendal is different – different to
the other Kendals anyway.
After all, he's the only one with brown hair
and brown eyes and what's more, he's taller
than his family, his friends and probably
everyone else in the entire world.

Big sister Jessie has made it clear just how
different Daniel is, by explaining that he is in
fact, an alien, kindly adopted by her parents.
Confused, Daniel turns to his
best friends, Eddie and Gordon the Geek,
for help. Together perhaps they can work out
where he really belongs.